KU-477-617

This book is about the city in which I live and is inspired by the legend of 'Black Donald.' Special thanks go to Harry Mould, who was kind enough to give me some insight into the nuts and bolts of theatre production in Edinburgh.

1

LEAVING

Allie had been walking for hours and her feet were bloody well killing her.

She'd already told herself, miles back, that she should have changed into more sensible shoes before she left, but she'd been too angry to think about anything practical. She'd been fuming! She'd gone straight upstairs to her bedroom to throw a few bits and pieces of clothing into her rucksack and she'd been thinking, I'll show them. I'll show them all! Then she'd put on her coat and marched straight downstairs and out of the front door, slamming it hard behind her, wanting her mother to know exactly what she was doing. She'd marched along the garden path, half-expecting the door to open and for Mum to shout after her, 'And where the hell d'you think you're going, Alison Lawrence?'

But Mum had either been calling her bluff or hadn't heard the slam of the door over the sound of Radio Two spilling from the speakers in the kitchen. Allie had made it to the end of the street unchallenged, then took the left turn onto the main road. She'd walked briskly through the village, not seeing a single person she recognised, and that suited her just fine, because the last thing she wanted right then was to talk to one of her so-called friends; the same friends who couldn't wait to tell her about Brandon – and what had happened between him and Jade at the party.

Oh, yes, they'd had a field day with that, hadn't they? They'd been virtually falling over each other in their haste to spill their guts over all the sordid details. Well, she'd told Brandon where he could go, and as for her 'friends', they wouldn't be laughing so loudly when they heard that she'd run away from home!

Pretty soon, she'd left civilisation behind her and was striking out along the endless straight run of the tarmac highway between ranks of silent green trees. Occasional cars rolled past her in the fading light of the afternoon.

As she walked, the argument replayed itself in her head. It had started innocently enough, with Mum asking a simple question.

'How do you feel about shepherd's pie?'

'Huh?'

'For tonight's dinner. I thought…'

'Whatever! Who cares?'

Mum frowning then, hands on hips. 'Allie, you've got to pull yourself together. You've been wandering around the house these past two days like a bear with a sore head.'

'Well, what do you expect?'

'Look, I understand you're put out, but…'

'Put out? Is that what you think? I'm more than 'put out,' Mother. I'm mad. Jade's supposed to be my best friend, for God's sake and she went behind my back. And it's your fault. You and Dad.'

'What on earth do you mean?'

'You wouldn't let me go to that party, would you? You said I had to stay home and revise. If I'd been there…'

'Allie, there are more important things than boyfriends. You've got exams coming up. You need to put your head down and do some work for once in your life. You can't expect to get anywhere if you don't put in the effort. I know you have this… ridiculous notion about acting, but… well, if you have the right grades, you'll get into a good university. And they're sure to have some kind of drama club there.'

'A club? You don't get it, do you? This isn't just a hobby. This is something I really want to do with my life. Miss Marchmont said…'

'Miss Marchmont! What does she know? And honestly, think about it for a moment! How would you even make a living? Goodness me, you can't boil an egg without instructions. And as for this thing with Brandon, well, it's not as if it was going anywhere, is it? There are plenty more fish in the sea.'

And Allie had snapped. She'd walked out. She'd walked out and she didn't care what anyone said, she wasn't going back, not for anything.

Only now it was starting to get dark, the slow lazy twilight of mid summer gathering around her and the ranks of trees on either side of the highway seemed darker, more impenetrable than they had before. It was still more than thirty miles to Perth, the nearest town of any size. She began to ask herself if she wouldn't have done better to plan this. She'd brought no food for her journey and when she put a hand into the pocket of her raincoat, she found that she only had a few coins to her name; she hadn't even thought to bring the debit card with which her scant savings could be accessed – not that fifty quid was going to go very far in her quest for superstardom, but still, it would have been something. It would have been better than… she took out the change and counted it in mounting disbelief – two pounds and forty-three pence.

She shook her head. 'Idiot,' she hissed.

Then she took her phone from the other pocket and

clicked it on. It had, she saw, exactly three percent of battery left. And of course, she'd forgotten to pick up her charger before she left the house. 'Idiot, idiot, IDIOT!'

She thought again about turning back, retracing her steps to the little two up, two down house that had been her home for the past sixteen years; thought about it and instantly dismissed the idea as she pictured her mother's triumphant smile as she dished out a plate of stodgy shepherd's pie at the kitchen table. Silly girl, she'd be thinking. Sees herself as all grown up but really she's still just a child.

Her dad would be a bit more sympathetic, of course, but in the end, he'd go along with Mum, just like he always did. 'I expect you're right, dear,' he'd say with that world-weary sigh of his. Then he'd take a seat in front of the television. 'Shall we see what's on the old goggle-box?'

No, Allie told herself. She was sticking to her guns. She even started walking faster along the road, wondering as she did so about trying to hitch a lift from one of the occasional cars that went by. She knew such a thing was sometimes done, she'd heard classmates boasting that they'd tried it, but the perceived wisdom seemed to be that it was a very bad thing to do, that a terrible fate lay in wait for those who were reckless enough to try it. You were liable to be picked up by a sex pest or a serial killer and that would be the end of you. But, on the other hand, she told herself, she'd be able to cover so much more ground if she did get a lift. She could be in Edinburgh by tonight...

'To do what?' she asked herself hopelessly. 'To do what exactly?'

Now the darkness was coming down properly and when she couldn't really make out the details on either side of the road, she felt considerably less sure of herself. If she did go back, she reasoned, would it really be so terrible? If nothing else, she'd have given her parents a good scare, shown them that she was not to be underestimated.

She reached a crossroads and for the first time since she'd walked out, she came to a halt. She stood there, looking around. Illuminated signs pointed in three directions. One told her that it was still thirty-one miles straight on to Perth. If she turned back now, she thought, she could be home by ten o clock. Yes, she'd get yelled at, but...

She turned her head as she became aware of two yellow lights approaching along the road behind her, moving slowly. She turned her face away, not wanting to be caught standing there, gawping like a fool at the oncoming vehicle – and then it occurred to her that it could very easily be her father, come looking for her in the family's Nissan – he'd be home from work by now. She thought about stepping quickly to the side of the road and concealing herself in the trees, but even as she thought about it, the car was slowing down and pulling to a halt alongside her. And now she *was* gawping. She couldn't help herself.

It was such a strange-looking car, a big old-fashioned sort of thing, the kind you only ever saw in old Hollywood movies, with glossy black bodywork and white-rimmed wheels. It had a black fabric roof, the sort that could be pulled back in hot weather allowing the occupants to bask in the sunshine. What did you call that? A convertible? The top was up, though, and as it drew to a halt, Allie saw the driver through the windscreen: an elderly man wearing a jacket and a peaked cap, his gaze fixed resolutely on the road ahead.

The vehicle finally came to a stop and now Allie saw the shadow of someone sitting in the back seat, staring intently at her through the window, but she couldn't see exactly who it was. Then the window was being slowly wound down and the person looking out at her was a handsome young boy of around her own age, she decided. He was dressed in a smart black jacket and he gazed out at her, a half-smile playing on his thin lips. There was a long silence as Allie stood and waited for him to speak and when he finally did, his voice was soft and refined, pitched somewhat lower than she might have expected.

'Can I drop you somewhere?' he asked her.

2

THE BOY IN THE CAR

Her first impulse was to say, 'Yes, please, that would be great', but she wasn't entirely convinced it was the right thing to do. She didn't know this boy – he was a complete stranger to her – and she thought, if she got into the car, then she would be abandoning the idea of changing her mind, throwing herself open to the possibility of things she did not really want to think about. She took a hesitant step closer and then another.

'I'm not sure,' she murmured.

This seemed to amuse the boy. His thin lips curved into a deeper smile. He was very good-looking, she thought and although she wasn't sure why, he didn't look like a local. The boys she knew were mostly sturdy shock-headed lads with ruddy faces and boring clothes. This one seemed cultured, and had what sounded like an Edinburgh accent.

'You're not sure I'm strong enough?' asked the boy.

She stared at him, not really understanding. 'I'm sorry?' she said.

'Strong enough to pick you up before I drop you,' he elaborated.

'Oh, no I…' She realised he'd been making a joke and felt her face flush. 'I… don't weigh all that much,' she said and then felt even more stupid. Why say that of all things? Idiot!

'Where are you headed?' asked the boy.

'Umm… well, Perth to start with and then–'

He leaned closer as though entranced. 'And then?' he echoed.

'Edinburgh?'

He nodded slowly as though considering her words. 'Good choice,' he said. 'I'd say that's definitely your best bet for acting work.'

She stared at him, open-mouthed. She couldn't have been more surprised if he'd slapped her.

'How… how did you…?'

'Well, it's all there, isn't it?' he said. 'It's in the way you carry yourself. Some people just have natural poise, don't you think?'

Allie didn't know what to say to that. She wasn't entirely sure what 'poise' meant, but she did think that he didn't sound like any boy she'd ever spoken to before. She took another step closer, intrigued. Now she was right beside the car.

'Where are you going?' she asked him.

'Perth,' he said. 'And Edinburgh.' A pause. 'Eventually.'

She frowned. 'Eventually?' she repeated.

'Well, we've driven quite a distance already tonight. I'm feeling rather tired. I thought perhaps I might call in somewhere first. You know, for a wee bite to eat. I wonder if you're hungry?' Again, he gave her that knowing smile. 'Don't worry,' he said. 'It won't be shepherd's pie.'

And again, Allie felt her jaw drop. She made a conscious effort to close it.

'Oh, well, I don't know.' She leaned to the side to look at the driver. All she could see was the back of his head, his unusually pronounced ears silhouetted against the glow of the windscreen, which was illuminated by the car's headlamps. 'Does your father think that's a good idea?' she asked.

Now the boy did laugh, a brief mocking chuckle. 'Do you hear that, Tam?' he asked the driver. 'She thinks you're my father!'

The driver didn't reply but perhaps his head nodded slightly.

'My chauffeur has no thoughts on the subject,' said the boy. 'His job is to take me wherever I wish to go. And whoever I care to take with me.'

Now Allie really did feel stupid. Her cheeks burned. She leaned in a little closer and realised that in the uncertain light she had been quite mistaken. This wasn't a boy at all, but rather, a young man, perhaps in his early twenties. 'Oh,' she said. 'I'm sorry, I didn't realise...'

For the first time, he looked impatient. 'Well, look here, Allie, are you getting in or not? I really would like to be on my way.'

She narrowed her eyes suspiciously.

'How did you know my name?' she demanded. 'I never told you.'

'True,' said the man. 'However, since it is embroidered on the bag on your back, I simply deduced that it must be your name.' He appeared to consider for a moment. 'Perhaps it's just the name of the bag,' he said.

This amused Allie. He talked strangely, she thought, not like anybody she'd ever spoken to before. 'Oh that, it's just... well, my mum embroidered my name on the bag and I suppose I only use it because I don't want to upset her.'

He smiled. 'How very considerate of you,' he said. 'Well, look, I don't want to seem brusque, but time is moving on and I really do need to get going. So make your mind up, please. Are you in or are you out?'

Allie hesitated again and the man turned to look at his chauffer. 'Drive on,' he said and Tam revved the engine.

And in that instant, Allie reached out impulsively and opened the door. Astonished by her own boldness, she looked into the interior of the car. It seemed cavernous inside. There was a long leather seat on which the man sat and another one facing him, just a couple of feet away. Allie settled herself awkwardly onto the opposite seat, holding her short dress down with one hand, knowing how it sometimes rode up in such circumstances, but the man didn't seem to take any notice. She saw now that what she had thought was a jacket was in fact a long, black satin coat. Was he a Goth or something? He reached out and pulled the door shut and it made a reassuringly deep clunking sound, quite unlike the tinny clank of the family's Nissan.

'Home,' he said and Tam put the car into gear. It moved smoothly away from the kerb and along the road, its engine barely making a sound.

There was a long silence then. Allie was aware that the man was looking at her intently as though expecting her to say something.

'So… er… where is home?' she asked, when she felt the silence had lasted long enough.

'Just along the road a little way,' said the man. 'It's nothing special, really, but we're comfortable there.'

'We?' she prompted him. 'You mean, you and your family?'

He didn't say anything to that.

'And do you have a name?' asked Allie. 'Well, of course you do, you must have, everyone has a name! But what I mean is… what is it?'

He seemed to take a long time to answer that question, as though he wasn't quite sure what to say.

'I've been known to answer to Donald,' he said.

For some reason that made her laugh and he did a strange thing. He tilted his head slightly to one side, as though intrigued.

'Why do you laugh?' he asked her.

'Oh, I'm sorry, it's just that you don't strike me as a Donald.'

'Do I not?'

'No! That's an old man's name. I think I have an Uncle Donald tucked away somewhere. He plays the accordion in a celidh band.'

'I must confess I'm less keen on it than I used to be,' he said. 'Ever since that shock-headed clown in America came along and turned it into a dirty word.' He seemed to ponder for a moment. 'Call me Nick,' he suggested. 'A lot of people seem to.' He scowled. 'I don't know why. I never asked them.'

'I don't expect you did,' said Allie, puzzled by his reply. 'Anyway, Nick is a much cooler name.'

'Do you think so?' He looked thoughtful again. 'Perhaps I should get a bag like yours, with "Nick" embroidered on it. What do you think?'

'I suppose you could,' she told him. 'I mean, boys have bags, don't they? I don't think I've seen many with their names on them, though.'

'Me neither,' he admitted. He seemed disappointed at the thought. 'Hardly seems fair. So, where are you from, Allie?'

'Oh, somewhere back down the ways,' she said, trying to be as mysterious as he had. For some reason, she felt suddenly more confident. 'Killiecrankie,' she said and smirked. 'Stupid name, isn't it?'

'I suppose. Actually, I've been there once or twice.'

'Oh? What were you doing in Killiecrankie?' asked Allie.

'Fishing,' he said, and left it at that.

'Where can you fish in Killiecrankie?' she asked him.

'Wherever you want,' he said with a shrug of his shoulders. 'Wherever there's something worth catching.'

'I've always called it Glum,' said Allie. 'The town of Glum.' She remembered an old joke her father delighted in telling. 'It's the kind of place where they don't bury the dead. They stand them up in bus shelters.' She grinned but Nick just looked wistful.

'Sounds like my kind of town,' he said.

Baffled, she turned her head to look out of the window. It was completely dark out there now and she could barely make out any detail.

'You could be taking me anywhere,' she observed and then was shocked at herself for saying such a thing. She made an attempt to gather her thoughts. 'So… is it far? To where we're going?'

'Not really,' said Nick. 'We'll only call in there for a while. And how long we stay rather depends on you.'

'What do you mean?' she asked him.

'Depends on whether or not you're hungry.' He smiled. 'I expect you must be. After all, it isn't every day a girl runs away from home.'

She actually gasped at that. 'I never said I'd run away from anywhere!' she protested.

'No, of course not,' he agreed. 'That would be a strange thing to admit to. But nevertheless, I somehow think you have.'

'What makes you say that?'

He shrugged. 'Call it intuition,' he said. 'I've a nose for

these things.' He made a show of leaning forward in his seat and sniffing the air ostentatiously.

'That's ridiculous,' she told him. 'What does somebody who's run away from home smell like?'

He sniffed again. 'Vanilla soap,' he said quietly. 'Apple shampoo. And a wee splash of your mother's Chanel No 5. She knows you take it, by the way. But she lets it go unchallenged. She doesn't want to cause a fuss.'

'This is beginning to feel very odd,' she warned him. 'I'm thinking about asking you to stop the car.'

He spread his hands. His expression seemed to suggest that it was no skin off his nose if she did. 'Not a problem,' he assured her. 'Awkward place to stop, mind you. Out in the middle of nowhere. I wouldn't fancy it, not on a dark night like this.' He smiled, a disarming smile that despite her reservations sent a strange thrill through her. He was incredibly good-looking, especially when he smiled. 'I was right about the perfume though, wasn't I?'

She couldn't help feeling amused by the observation. 'It's true,' she admitted. She gave him a stern look. 'Don't tell my mum,' she said.

'How could I?' he asked her. 'I've never met her.'

The car turned off the main road and Allie turned her head to look out of the window. She had an impression of a narrow, winding lane, flanked on either side by rows of trees. She caught just a fleeting glimpse of the full moon through overhanging foliage, floating in the sky like a Chinese paper lantern. 'Where are we going exactly?' she asked again.

'My place,' he said. 'Don't worry, I'm not a murderer or anything.'

'That's good to hear,' she said. 'Does "your place" have a name?'

13

He seemed to consider for a moment. 'Kevin,' he said.

'Very funny. No, I mean, what's it called?'

'It's called "Nick's House".'

She was starting to feel irritated by his mocking tone. 'Seriously,' she insisted. 'What's the address?'

'It doesn't really have one,' he said, bafflingly. 'Not one that anyone would remember.'

At that instant the car made another left turn and came to an abrupt halt. 'Anyway,' he added, 'as it turns out, we're already there.' He reached out a hand and opened the door, then sat looking at her, as though expecting her to make the first move. She got out of the car and found herself standing on a gravel drive. In front of her stood a massive, crumbling, three storey edifice made from smooth grey stone. She stared at it in amazement. It seemed to soar into the air above her, looking like something from a fairy tale: all turrets and towers and windows, from which not a single light could be seen.

'Is there anyone else here?' she asked worriedly.

'Of course,' he assured her. 'Always.' He nodded towards the house. 'It's not much,' he said, 'but we call it home.' Now he followed her out of the car and as he stepped out, he placed one hand gently on her arm. She almost jumped out of her skin. It felt as though a strange warmth was flowing from his hand, a powerful, melting feeling. He had picked up a cane from somewhere, a long black one with an elaborate silver top. He took a couple of steps towards the house, slamming the car door behind him and she went with him.

'How long have you lived here?' she asked.

'As long as I can remember,' he said.

'You must be very well off to live in a place like this.'

'Well off?' he murmured.

'Yes, you know. Rich.'

'We've never gone short of anything we wanted,' he admitted.

The car drove around the side of the house, out of sight.

'Where's he off to?' murmured Allie.

'To the garage,' said Nick. He indicated the massive black front door and a short flight of grey marble steps leading up to it. They went up them and as they got to the top, a light snapped on within and the door swung silently open. A woman stood there, looking out at them, a tall middle-aged woman dressed in black. She had thin, pale features and small dark eyes. Her grey hair was tied in a tight bun at the back of her head. She examined Allie coldly for a moment and then her gaze moved sideways to Nick.

'Good evening, Agatha,' said Nick. 'I've brought a guest for dinner.'

She seemed immediately reassured, her lips curving into a polite smile.

'Oh, very good, sir,' she said. 'Nice to have you back.' She stepped aside and bowed her head, revealing a hallway that seemed bigger than Allie's entire house. Allie glanced uncertainly at Nick and he smiled at her. 'Well, don't stand on ceremony,' he said. 'In you go.'

She nodded and stepped over the threshold into the house. Nick followed her into the hall and the heavy door closed behind them.

3

ICE CREAM & SALTED CARAMEL SAUCE

Allie followed Agatha down the hallway and Nick strolled along a short distance behind them. Open doorways led off on either side into big, dark rooms. Allie glanced into one of them as she passed. It had huge leaded windows and shafts of moonlight were spilling in through the dusty glass. It looked as though nobody had been in there for ages, Allie thought. The floor was littered with dead leaves and she had a brief impression of a mouldering table, littered with cobweb-strewn candelabra and lined with tattered chairs. She suppressed a shiver. She was beginning to wish she'd never climbed into Nick's car, but it was a little late for regrets.

They moved on along the hallway.

'We'll dine in the big room,' announced Nick cheerfully, presumably for Agatha's benefit. 'Ask Julia if she'd be kind enough to join us, would you?'

'I will, sir,' said Agatha over her shoulder and carried on walking.

'Allie, this way, please.' Allie paused and turned to see that Nick was heading back the way they had just come. She followed him and he turned left into the large room she had glanced into. She was aware, as he disappeared from view, of lights coming on within. She followed him inside and stood for a moment, gazing around in astonishment.

Her first glimpse of the place had been completely mistaken, she realised. It was actually spotlessly clean and opulently furnished. One end of the long wooden dining table was already set for three people. There were expensive-looking silver salvers, white porcelain plates and gleaming wine glasses. The wooden floor had been polished until it shone and there was no sign of the leaves she thought she'd seen before. In an open fireplace, a log fire blazed cheerfully. She looked at Nick in surprise.

'But... I could have sworn...'

He looked at her, his eyebrows raised. 'What?'

'That this room was...' She shook her head. No, that was ridiculous. It had looked different in the darkness, that was all. 'This is lovely,' she said.

'Please have a seat,' he suggested. He waved her into an elegantly carved wooden chair and when she had settled herself and set her rucksack down on the floor, he went around to the far side of the table, removed his coat and slung it carelessly over the back of another chair. Then he sat himself down with a sigh of content. 'Red or white?' he asked, gesturing to a couple of open bottles standing on the table. She gave him a look and he corrected himself. 'I mean, lemonade or cola?'

She opted for cola and he picked up the red wine bottle and started to fill her glass. She was about to object but then saw that what was actually flowing into the glass was definitely cola. She lifted her glass and took a cautious sip, just to confirm that it really was what it looked like.

'Are you some kind of a magician?' she asked him. He was pouring a blood red liquid into his own glass now, and, it struck her, he was still using the same bottle.

He shrugged. 'I've been called many things,' he admitted. 'Not all of them friendly. Never a magician, though. I think I rather like it.' He smiled his handsome smile and set down the bottle. 'Now, what do you fancy for your dinner?' he asked her. He took hold of the handle of a silver salver. 'How about a spot of venison?'

She grimaced. 'Not sure I fancy that,' she said.

He lifted the lid to reveal a haunch of glistening red meat on a plate. 'When Tam's not driving me around in the limousine, he's a dead shot with a rifle. There's plenty of these lads in the woods hereabouts.'

Allie crinkled her nose in disgust. 'I'm not eating that,' she protested. 'It would feel like eating Bambi.'

'No, quite right, absolutely disgusting!' He replaced the lid and reached for another handle. 'Perhaps a spot of freshly caught Scottish salmon?' he suggested, lifting this lid and showing three whole fish, their heads still on, lying in a row on a bed of spinach. They looked, Allie thought, faintly astonished to be there.

Again, she grimaced. 'Not really keen on fish,' she said.

He shook his head, replaced the lid. 'Oh, you're a picky one aren't you?' he chided her. He considered for a moment. 'Well, let's see now. If you could have whatever you fancy right this moment, what would it be?'

'Anything?' she asked him.

'Anything at all.'

She thought for a moment. 'Maccy D's and chips,' she said.

He looked puzzled by this. 'Maccy D's?' he echoed

'It's a burger,' she explained. 'You know, a beef burger in a bun. With French fries?'

'Ah!' He grinned. 'Of course. Well, as luck would have it–' He lifted the lid of a third salver to reveal several large burgers, surrounded by glistening mounds of chips. 'Please help yourself,' he suggested.

She stared at him for a few moments and then took him at his word, heaping her plate with food, realising that it was hours past her usual mealtime and that all that walking had worked up quite an appetite. He just sat there watching her. 'Are you not eating anything?' she asked him.

He shook his head. 'You go right ahead,' he told her. 'Eating's not really my thing. I'll just watch.' He leaned back in his chair with a smile.

Allie took a bite from her burger. It was, she decided, delicious, quite the nicest burger she could ever remember tasting, the meat moist and succulent. It had just the right amount of lettuce, just enough ketchup.

Nick took a gulp from his glass and smacked his lips. 'Tomato juice,' he assured her, but somehow she doubted that was true. 'Ah,' he said, looking towards the doorway. 'Here's Julia.' He smiled and raised his glass.

Allie turned her head to look. The middle-aged woman who had just swept into the room was quite beautiful, she thought; tall and slender with long, straight black hair that hung to her shoulders. She was dressed in a dark red silk dress that clung to her curves like a sheath and exactly matched the shade of lipstick on her full, beautifully-shaped mouth. Her large piercing eyes were a vivid green and their gaze lingered on Allie for a moment before flicking across to her companion.

'Hello, Mother,' said Nick.

She stood for a moment, gazing at him. 'Really?' she murmured.

'Really,' he said. 'Allow me to introduce a new friend, Allie.'

Julia studied Allie doubtfully for a moment and then moved politely forward and extended a hand. 'Any friend of my son's,' she finished and took a seat beside Allie. She studied the array of plates and dishes in front of her for a moment and then her gaze moved over to the bottles. 'I'll have white,' she said.

Nick picked up another bottle and filled a crystal glass with colourless liquid. She nodded her thanks, picked up the glass and took an appreciative sip. She looked at the food on Allie's plate and smiled, seemingly amused. 'So… what are we eating tonight?' she asked.

'It's Maccy D's,' Nick told her. 'Quite the thing these days, or so I'm told. Luckily, it was exactly what Allie fancied.'

'That's nice.' Julia smiled. 'It's always good to be able to offer guests a little of what they fancy.'

'Aren't you going to eat something, Mrs…?' Allie realised she didn't know the woman's surname.

'Please call me Julia. And I must confess, I have no appetite whatsoever this evening. But do enjoy your meal. It looks… so unusual.' She gazed serenely across the table at Nick. 'Now,' she said, 'I feel sure that somebody's going to tell me what's happening.'

Nick smiled and took another sip of his red drink. 'Well, Mother… there I was, driving home from my wee adventure in Killiecrankie, when who should I see standing at the crossroads, but Allie here. It was getting rather late and she seemed to be far from home, so I thought the very least I could do was stop and offer her a lift.'

'Ever the gentleman,' observed Julia and Allie thought there was something faintly mocking in her tone.

'One tries to do one's bit. Anyway, we had only gone a short distance when I learned that she was heading for Edinburgh and naturally, as I'm planning a trip there myself, tomorrow, it only seemed right that I should offer to take her along with me.'

Julia nodded. She turned her head to look at Allie. 'And what's waiting for you in Edinburgh?' she asked.

'Oh, er… well, I haven't really got that much of a plan,' admitted Allie.

'You surprise me,' said Julia. 'Do go on.'

' It's going to sound crazy, but, I was thinking about…' She broke off, suddenly uncertain about whether she should say more.

'Yes, my dear?' Julia prompted her. 'Speak up.'

'I have this idea that I'd like to… act.'

There was a brief silence while her two companions digested the remark. Then Nick leaned forward, a triumphant expression on his face. 'I knew it!' he exclaimed. 'I absolutely knew it!' He looked at Allie. 'Didn't I say just before you got into the car, that you have all the poise of a performer? And didn't I add that Edinburgh would be your best bet if you wanted to follow that profession?'

'Er… you did say something like that,' admitted Allie. 'Which I thought was kind of weird.'

'No, not weird at all! It's only common sense. And it makes all this so perfect. You see, Allie, that's what I do.'

'What you do?'

'For a living. I manage people's careers.'

Allie put down her half-finished burger and stared at him open-mouthed. 'For a living? But… excuse me, you… you don't look old enough.'

He looked hurt by the remark. 'Now you've cut me to the quick,' he said.

'Well I'm sorry, but how old are you? Twenty, twenty-one? Most of the managers I've seen in films and TV shows – well, they're older than that.'

'Trust me, Allie. Age is not a problem. Shall I tell you why?'

She looked at him doubtfully. 'Okay,' she said.

'Because acting is a young person's profession. The world belongs to the young! Nobody wants to hear some old fogey intoning his deathless Shakespearean prose any more.' He pointed a finger at Allie. 'I look at you and I see the next big thing. And if I say to you, Allie, the word "actress"...'

'Bit sexist,' muttered Allie.

He hesitated, looking puzzled. 'I'm sorry?' he said. 'Sexist?' His baffled expression suggested that he was unfamiliar with the term.

'Nobody uses that word any more,' she told him. 'Now we just say "actors" for both sexes. Male actors and female actors.'

'Er... yes, yes, of course. Quite right.' He made an effort to recover his train of thought. 'So, as I was saying... if I say the words "female actor" to you, whose face do you see in your mind's eye?'

Allie thought for a moment. 'Erm... well, I suppose... somebody like... Roxanne Walsh?' she ventured.

'Exactly!' Nick and Julia exchanged brief looks before he continued. 'Roxanne... Walsh! Yes! And... how old is she, may I ask?'

'I'm not sure. I think she's in her early thirties, now, but she was only eighteen when she started. She was in that sitcom on the telly, you know, the one set in a school? She's dead famous, won all kinds of theatre awards.'

'Well, there you go!' Nick lifted his hands to make a dramatic gesture. 'Just think what a wonderful advantage we'd have.' He lifted his voice as though making a grand announcement. 'Ladies and gentlemen, introducing the new star of stage and screen: Allie Lawrence, sweet sixteen!' He looked pleased with himself. 'Must make a note of that,' he murmured.

Again, there was that thing of knowing more than he should. 'I'm pretty sure I didn't tell you my age,' Allie pointed out.

'No. But it's obvious, isn't it? You look sixteen. You act sixteen. And that, my dear Allie, is going to be your USP.'

'My what?

'Your Unique Selling Proposition!' He looked ridiculously pleased with himself. 'Just a term we managers use,' he explained. 'The thing that will give you an edge over the competition. And in your case, it's your age. Now, what do you say? I'm feeling positive about this. Shall we make a deal?'

'Umm...' Allie looked hopefully at Julia who seemed to understand.

'Don't rush the girl,' she advised Nick. 'This is a big decision for her.'

'Nonsense! I'm offering to make her a star. That's all there is to it.'

Allie picked up a chip from her plate and stirred it thoughtfully through a pool of ketchup. 'How would it work exactly?' she asked.

'Well, it's very straightforward, Allie. I've done it many times. I would draw up a contract, which you would sign. I would get you to a certain point in your career...'

He thought for a moment. 'Let me see now, what would seem a reasonable position for you to be in? Ah! How about this? I will obtain for you the starring role in a new play in one of Edinburgh's leading theatres. At which point, I will consider my work done.'

'You make it sound easy,' observed Allie.

'I certainly don't mean to,' said Nick. 'It's going to take a lot of work and a whole lot of money.' He rubbed his index finger and thumb together in the age-old gesture.

Allie slipped a hand into her pocket and pulled out the change she knew was there. She set it down on the table in front of her.

'What's that?' asked Julia, puzzled.

'It's all I've got in the world,' Allie told her. 'Two pounds and forty-three pence.' She looked at Nick. 'So I really don't think this is going to work.'

Nick made a dismissive gesture. 'You won't be required to pay anything,' he assured her. 'Leave the money side of things to me. I'll take care of everything for now and I'll take my commission, later.'

'And how much is that going to be?' asked Allie, doubtfully.

'The standard agency fee,' said Nick, as though it was of little consequence. 'Don't you worry about minor details. I'll spend tonight drawing up the contract and you can sign it in the morning.'

'In the morning?' murmured Allie.

'Well, it's getting rather late for a long drive, don't you think? Better if you get some rest tonight and we'll head off tomorrow.'

There was a short silence. Allie couldn't help asking herself where she was going to be sleeping. But Julia seemed to sense her discomfort.

'I'll have Agatha make up the guest room,' suggested Julia, getting up from her seat. 'Don't worry, my dear, you'll be perfectly comfortable there.' But she paused and looked at Allie intently. 'You must think very carefully before you sign,' she said. 'It's a serious commitment, this. Not to be undertaken lightly.'

Nick gave her a withering look. 'Hadn't you better go and organise the sleeping arrangements... Mother?'

Julia nodded, turned away and went obediently out of the room.

There was another silence then. Allie gazed across the table at Nick. 'You're sure you know what you're doing?' she asked him.

He scoffed. 'Of course! I've been managing people's careers for a long time. Trust me.' He waved a hand at Allie's half-eaten meal. 'Have you had enough to eat?' he asked her. 'Would you like something to finish off? Something sweet?'

'Not unless you've got vanilla ice cream with salted caramel sauce,' she said. 'It's my favourite.'

He hesitated for just a moment. 'As it happens...' He lifted the lid of another platter and there was exactly that, heaped into a sundae glass, complete with fresh strawberries and a wafer. She stared at it in disbelief.

'This is starting to get a wee bit scary,' she murmured, but she reached out, took the glass and tried some. It tasted like a mouthful of heaven. 'I could get used to this,' she murmured.

'Hmm. Well, I wouldn't get too used to it,' he advised her. 'You'll need to keep your figure if you're going to be a successful actor.'

'But... I'm not being funny...'

'Go on.'

'You haven't even seen me act. You don't even know if I'm any good.'

He nodded, as though the idea hadn't even occurred to him. 'Fair point,' he admitted. 'That would be a disaster, wouldn't it? I sign you to a contract and you can't act for toffee. Well, let's see, shall we?' He made a theatrical flourish. 'Consider this your audition. Give me something.'

She stared at him. 'Like what?' she murmured.

'Your showpiece. Every actor has a showpiece, surely?'

'What, here? Now?'

25

'Of course! You'll have to audition for directors, after all. And they aren't going to give you any time to prepare yourself. They aren't going to say, "give me a ring when you're in the mood". Just give me the piece you'll do for them, whenever they ask.'

'Oh – well, OK.' She thought for a moment and then stood up, telling herself that she'd do the same thing she'd performed for Miss Marchmont when she'd auditioned for the school play. It wasn't ideal, but she hadn't prepared anything else, so she supposed it would have to do.

'This,' she said, 'is Abigail Williams from *The Crucible*. You do know the play, I suppose?'

He smirked. 'Of course,' he said. 'And I knew the author.'

She gave him a baffled look. 'You knew Arthur Miller?' she murmured.

'Er… no! I meant to say that I knew the author of the recent adaptation that played in London.' He smiled. 'A huge success,' he added. 'Won a whole clutch of awards. And turned the young lady who played the same role into a major star.'

She waited for him to say more, but he didn't elaborate, so she stepped back a few paces from the table, cleared her mind of all thought and then began her piece, her favourite scene from the school production in which she had recently starred. It was the scene where Abigail speaks to John Proctor about the witchcraft rituals she has recently taken part in; and where she mentions that she and Proctor have had a secret affair.

Allie affected a faraway look as she recited the words, aware as she did so that Nick had taken a small leatherbound book from his pocket, opened it and was gazing at the pages, as though in deep thought. It was only a short piece and, despite his apparent disinterest, she managed to keep going to the end. When she'd finished, he looked up at her, as though surprised that it was already over.

'Bravo,' he said. He put down the book and brought his hands together in soft applause. 'Superb.'

'Really?' She didn't feel entirely convinced.

'Oh yes,' he assured her. 'Quite marvellous. You captured Alison perfectly.'

'It's Abigail,' she corrected him.

'Quite. It was uncanny. You could have been her.'

'So… I passed the audition?'

'With flying colours! I'm convinced that you're the best actor I've seen in a long time. And trust me, I've seen a lot. Now, sit down and finish your ice cream,' he suggested. She did as he said, stirring the contents around with her spoon, but she was feeling too nervous now to be hungry.

'You don't have anything to say about my performance?' she prompted him. 'Any advice?'

He seemed to consider for a moment, before replying.

'I think… I think there's a rare quality in you, Allie. An inner strength. That is something I can work with. Oh, yes. Some people think that you can learn to be a great actor, but I believe it has to be there already, deep inside you and bursting to come out. My plan is simply to release that talent. The best way to do that is for you to trust me.'

'Who says I don't trust you?'

Nick smiled, those dark eyes challenging her.

'Allie, I know you don't. And why would you? You've only just met me. But don't worry, that's something I intend to work on.' He reached out and placed a hand on hers and once again she felt an unexpected thrill, like a bolt of pure electricity jolting through her. It made her feel somehow sensual, as though she was relaxing in a hot, perfumed bath.

'I want to trust you,' she said quietly.

'Then just allow yourself to,' he murmured. He was staring intently into her eyes now and she felt that luxurious warmth radiating through her. It was as though he could see deep within her, to her deepest, darkest desires. 'Just stop resisting me and everything will be fine,' he said.

Just then, she became aware of a presence behind her and, turning, she saw the angular shape of Agatha standing in the doorway, her pale face expressionless.

'Please, sir,' she said, 'the guest bedroom is all prepared.'

'Thank you, Agatha.' Nick looked at Allie and gave her that knowing smile. 'You must be very tired,' he said. 'Why don't you go on up to your room and I'll get the contract prepared for the morning, before we leave.'

'Leave?' she murmured.

'For Edinburgh,' he said. 'That's where you were headed, right?' He went back to studying his little book. Allie nodded. She stood up from the table.

'I'll say goodnight then,' she told him.

He looked up for a moment as though he'd already forgotten her. 'Yes,' he said. 'Good night, Allie. Sleep well.'

She turned away from the table and followed Agatha out into the hall and up the broad sweep of the staircase.

4

SWEET DREAMS

The bedroom looked like something out of a history book, Allie thought, so different from the modest little bedroom she slept in at home. The only light here came from a couple of candles standing at either end of a white marble fireplace. They illuminated the interior with a dull, flickering glow that threw restless shadows across the carved wooden panels lining the walls. There was a big, four-poster bed, hung with weird drapes that were like old tapestries and there was some big, heavy-looking furniture made from dark, glossy wood: a wardrobe, a chest of drawers and a dressing table. The creaky floorboards had a garishly patterned rug laid across them, which depicted a hunting scene. Men with rifles were pursuing what looked like a huge black wolf up the side of a steep hill. Allie moved closer to the bed. A white nightdress had been laid out on the crimson silk coverlet, its short sleeves spread out on either side. Agatha waved a hand at it.

'The Mistress picked that out for you to wear,' she said. 'I'd say it's about your size.' She waved a hand around the room. 'I trust you'll be comfortable here.' She indicated a metal button set into the wall beside the bed. 'If you should require anything, anything at all, just press that button and I shall attend you.'

'Er... thanks.' Agatha spoke like something out of a

history book, too, Allie decided. 'I will. What time do people get up in the morning?'

Agatha looked mystified by the question. 'Whenever they feel ready to face the day,' she said 'Well, miss, I'll bid you goodnight.' And with that she left the room, closing the door behind her.

Allie walked over to the window and stared out into the darkness. Below her, she could see a garden and what looked like an orchard of fruit trees, swaying rhythmically in the wind. Just then, a figure walked between the trees, a big, solid shape, a man wearing a peaked cap. She recognised Tam, the chauffeur. What was he doing wandering about in the dark like that? Even as she thought it, he paused and looked up towards her window, his face impassive. His eyes briefly reflected the light from the window, giving them a ghoulish glow. His mouth widened into a strange grin. Allie stepped quickly back, not wanting him to see her standing there. She pulled her phone from her pocket and switched it on, noting that the battery was now on one percent and that there were around a dozen missed calls and text messages from her mother – also plenty of texts from her so-called friends. She imagined her mother frantically calling a list of numbers, asking if anybody knew where her daughter was and them texting her, fascinated to know what was going on.

Allie clicked on her contacts list and chose 'Home'. There was the familiar number; all she had to do was press 'call'. But still she hesitated. If she did phone, what would she tell her parents? She didn't even know where she was! Of course, it was possible to trace a phone, she had seen that done in films. All she would need to do would be to leave the device switched on and the police would be able to home right in on her.

But then she thought about what Nick had said.

I will obtain for you the starring role in a new play in one of Edinburgh's leading theatres.

He had said it with such certainty, as though achieving such an outcome would present absolutely no problem for him, as though it was the easiest thing in the world. And she genuinely couldn't think of anything she wanted more. She itched for it. She could almost taste the flavour of success on her tongue, as sweet and enticing as the ice cream and salted caramel sauce Nick had offered her.

She thought about how odd her situation was. Nick, appearing out of the darkness like that. Nick, who seemed to know so much about her, as if the two of them were old friends... Nick who could seemingly make impossible things happen.

She stared at her phone again and raised her thumb to click 'call'. And in that same instant the screen went black as the phone died. She shook her head, let out a sigh of relief, acknowledging that the decision had been taken away from her and that she was somehow glad of it. She slid the phone back into her pocket, then turned towards the bed and stood for a moment, looking uncertainly down at the white nightdress, which seemed like something from another age, so different from the comfy fleece pyjamas she wore at home. She took off her coat, her shoes, her T-shirt and jeans, then pulled the nightdress over her head. It fit perfectly. She walked across to the wardrobe mirror and inspected herself for a moment, thinking that she looked like something from a child's fairy story. She went over to the huge bed and pulled back the covers, then slipped between the red satin sheets and leaned back against her pillows. She lay there, gazing thoughtfully around the room.

There came the sound of a gentle tapping on her door and she froze, gazed anxiously towards it. 'Who is it?' she asked.

'It's only Julia. May I come in for a moment?'

'Of course.' The door opened and Julia seemed to glide silently into the room. She came over and perched herself elegantly on the side of the bed. 'I wondered if there's anything else you need,' she asked.

'No, I'm... I'm fine,' said Allie, doubtfully. She thought for a moment. 'I don't suppose you have an iPhone charger?'

Julia looked at her blankly, as though she'd said, 'I don't suppose you have a rhinoceros?' She shook her head. 'I'm afraid not,' she said.

'But you must have some kind of a phone here,' insisted Allie.

'No. We don't hold with them,' said Julia. 'We've managed to resist all of that modern paraphernalia.' She gestured around. 'You'll probably have noticed there are no televisions here. No radios. That's the way we like it.'

'But Nick's supposed to be a manager, isn't he? How can he manage without a mobile?'

'There are ways and means,' Julia assured her, mysteriously. 'Nick's methods are... unconventional, but they do get results.' She smiled. 'Actually, to be fair to him, he is trying to modernise. You know, move with the times and all that. We've talked about it a lot, recently. He feels he's in danger of getting a little... out of touch.'

'Out of touch?' Allie struggled to follow the logic. 'But he's not more than a few years older than me, surely?'

'No, but he's surprisingly set in his ways. What you might call a traditionalist. It's all to do with his upbringing. He told me recently that he wants, more than anything else, to step into the twenty-first century.'

'Yeah, well, he should start by getting a mobile phone,' said Allie.

Julia smiled and studied her with interest. 'Is this the first time you've been away from home?' she asked.

'Of course not,' said Allie, scornfully, but it was a lie. 'I've had loads of trips away. Loads. With the... school and... with friends. My parents are cool with it, actually. They say it's good for me.'

Julia nodded. 'I see. And do you have a boyfriend?'

Allie scowled. 'I did have one. We went out for the best part of a year, but he turned out to be a liar, so I dumped him.'

'Oh dear. Was this recently?'

'It was just the other day, actually.'

'Then perhaps there's some chance of a reconciliation?'

'There's no chance,' Allie assured her. 'None at all. In fact, if I never see him again, it will be too soon.'

'I see. Well, of course, you must do what seems right. And... I wonder, have you had a chance to think about whether you want to sign Nick's contract?'

Allie frowned. 'It's all going a wee bit fast for me,' she said. 'I mean, what he said before. About "the usual agency fee". How much is this going to cost me? I don't have any money.'

'Oh, it's not about money,' Julia assured her. 'It's never been about that.' She waved a hand as if it was of no consequence. 'I'm sure Nick will explain everything fully in the morning. But, like I said, you should consider very carefully, before you make your mind up. It's a big decision.'

'Can he really do what he says?' Allie asked her. 'Like... get me the lead role in a play?'

Julia nodded. 'Of course,' she said. 'He wouldn't make

such a claim if he didn't believe he could do it.'

'So why do I get the feeling that you don't really want me to sign?'

'My dear girl, I have no feelings about it one way or the other. I just want you to be aware of how serious a commitment it is. You need to understand. I've seen plenty of others before you. Not just young girls, mind. Men and women of all ages, all denominations. Some of them were perfectly happy with the deal they made. Others... not so very much. Some came to resent Nick, to feel that he had tricked them.'

Allie frowned. 'Why? Didn't they get what he'd promised them?'

'Oh, they got everything they wanted.'

'So, why the disappointment?'

Julia seemed to consider the question for a long time.

'I suppose some people came to the realisation that what they thought they wanted wasn't as important as some other things.'

'Such as?'

Julia shrugged her narrow shoulders. 'Oh, you know. Health... happiness... security. That sort of thing.'

Allie snorted. 'I'm not bothered about any of that,' she said. 'I know what I want. It's what I've wanted since I was a wee girl. And anyway, what's the alternative? Staying in that dead end village, going to the same dead end school. Hoping that one day I'll meet the right boy, settle down and have half a dozen bairns? I'll be damned if I'll let that happen to me!'

Julia smiled ruefully. 'Would it really be so very awful?'

'It would be desperate. I want to make something of my life. I want to be somebody. You see, it's enough for my mum and dad. Just... rubbing along. Watching the telly, doing the dishes. Maybe having a takeaway on a Saturday night if they feel like really spoiling themselves...' She made a sound of exasperation. 'If I thought that was all I had to look forward to, I don't know what I'd do! No, I want to act. And I believe I can. Miss Marchmont says I have talent.'

Julia narrowed her eyes. 'Miss Marchmont?'

'My drama teacher at school. She's the one who cast me as the lead in the school play.' She made a face. 'I was playing Miss Hannigan in *Annie*, so... that wasn't such a big deal. But, for my drama exam, she got me to study the role of Abigail Williams in *The Crucible*.'

'Ah...'

'And, you know, honestly, I've never felt happier than when I'm speaking her lines. It just feels... right. Miss Marchmont says that acting's in my blood. She thinks I'm a natural. She actually said that to me once, during a break in rehearsals. She said, "Allie, you're a natural."'

'That's a rare accolade,' admitted Julia.

'And she chose me out of everyone who auditioned for the role of Miss Hannigan. That's more than twenty girls.'

'Yes.' Julia nodded. 'I can see that must have been... encouraging.'

There was another long silence, before Allie spoke again.

'I know that Nick is your son...' she began.

Julia leaned closer. 'Yes?'

'But... he's very strange, isn't he?'

'I suppose he is a bit unusual...'

'It's more than that. The way he talks, the things he does. He's not like anyone I've ever met before.'

'You're certainly not the first person to say that. Mind you, he would only see it as a compliment.'

'Is there... I mean, is there something wrong with him?'

'Wrong?' Julia looked slightly put out by the question. 'There's nothing wrong, Allie. He's just different. And, when all is said and done, he cannot help the way he is, can he?'

'No, I suppose not. But… it's kind of unsettling. I really don't know what he's all about.'

'Right now, he's putting all his efforts into making you a success. And believe me, if he says he can do it, you'd do well to believe him.' Julia stood up from the bed. 'Now, I really think I should let you get some sleep,' she announced. 'It's late and you have a journey to make tomorrow.' She drifted over to the fireplace. 'Shall I blow out these candles for you?'

'No!' The reply came out a little sharper than Allie had intended. 'No, please leave them on. If you don't mind.'

'Why would I mind?' murmured Julia. She studied Allie with interest. 'Are you afraid of the dark?'

'Er… no, not especially, But…'

'But it's always difficult when you're in an unfamiliar place. I completely understand. Good night, my dear. Sweet dreams.'

She moved past the foot of the bed in a swish of silk and then the door opened and closed and Allie was alone in the room. She lay there, propped up by her pillows, staring into the flickering gloom, trying to make sense of everything that had happened to her.

All in all, it was a long time before she slept that night and, when she finally did, she dreamed she was standing in the wings of a huge theatre, waiting for her cue to go on. When she looked to her right, she could see two women dressed in brightly-coloured gowns, talking intently to each other in loud voices. Beyond them, she could see the steeply inclined seats, packed with faceless people, watching the drama unfold, and she couldn't help but notice that the audience were dressed in old-style clothing: the men wearing satin jackets, powdered wigs on their heads, the women in more brightly-coloured silk gowns. When Allie heard the familiar line she'd been waiting for, 'Ah, here she comes now!', she stumbled reflexively out into the glare of the lights, and found to her dismay that she had completely forgotten her opening line and could only stand, gazing helplessly out at the crowd, her mouth opening and closing like a stranded fish.

5

BABETTE

She woke suddenly with the distinct feeling that she was no longer alone in the room. Her vision focused and she started violently as she registered that a face was staring intently at her, only inches away from her own. She almost cried out in terror, but then realised that the face belonged to a pale but pretty little girl, who was standing beside the bed. Her blonde hair was braided into two long plaits and she wore a white nightgown. She was hugging a rather tatty-looking doll to her chest.

'H… hello?' whispered Allie. She didn't really know what else to say.

'Hello,' said the little girl. She grinned, displaying a pronounced gap in her upper front teeth. Allie decided the girl could be no more than six or seven years old. She was studying Allie solemnly.

'Who are you?' the little girl whispered.

'Er, my name is Allie.'

The little girl nodded, her expression serious. 'I'm Babette,' she said. 'You're in my bed,' she added.

'Oh, am I? I'm sorry, I didn't know. This is where they put me.'

'I always sleep here,' continued Babette, reaching out a little hand to stroke the coverlet. 'But tonight my mummy woke me up and said I should let a guest use it instead.'

'Your mummy? Is that Julia?'

Babette nodded. 'I told her I wouldn't be able to sleep somewhere else but she said that we all have to make sacrifices sometimes.'

'I see. Well, I'm very sorry. If I'd known, I'd have asked to be put somewhere else. It's not nice to be thrown out of your bed.' Allie thought for a moment. 'So Nick must be your big brother?'

Babette didn't answer that, as though she hadn't really realised that it was meant to be a question. 'I'm very cold,' she said.

'I expect you must be,' agreed Allie. 'Would you like me to take you back to your room?'

Babette shook her head. 'Can I get in with you?' she asked. 'Please?'

Allie hesitated. She didn't like the idea at all and wondered how she could say that without upsetting the little girl. 'Well...' she began.

It was already too late. Babette had taken Allie's hesitancy as agreement and before she could stop the girl, she'd pulled back the covers and scrambled in beside her. 'Oh, Babette, I'm really not sure–'

But now Babette was cuddling up to her and Allie had to agree that the little girl did feel icy cold, as though the chill emanated from somewhere deep inside her. Allie looked hopefully towards the door, thinking that perhaps Julia might appear and take charge of her daughter, but it didn't happen. Allie looked down and saw that Babette's pale little features were gazing up at her with intense interest. Allie felt obliged to make some conversation. She lifted a hand and indicated the doll, an old-fashioned one with a rouged china face and green, staring eyes. 'So... who's this?' she inquired.

'This is Molly,' said Babette. 'She's very naughty.'

'Is she really?' Despite herself, Allie felt a smile twitching the corners of her mouth. 'What does she get up to?'

'Bad things,' said Babette, glumly. 'Very bad things.'

Allie's smile deepened. 'What kind of bad things?'

'Well,' Babette took a deep breath. 'She tells lies.'

'Does she really?' Allie shook her head. 'Surely not?'

'She does.'

Allie waved a finger in the doll's face. 'Molly, that is very naughty of you. You must make an effort to be better behaved.' She smiled at Babette. 'What else does she do?'

'Well, Mummy gave me a kitten to play with and I really, really, really liked that kitten.'

'Yes?' ventured Allie.

'And Molly killed it.'

Allie's smile faded.

'Oh, no, I don't think that can be right.'

'But she did.' Babette's expression was deadly serious. 'She thought I liked the kitten more than I liked her so she killed it.'

'But that couldn't happen, could it?' reasoned Allie.

'Ask her,' suggested Babette. 'Go on, just ask her.'

'No, that would be – I really don't want to.' Allie made an effort to change the subject. 'So, how old are you, Babette?'

There was a long silence as though the little girl was thinking carefully about it. 'I'm not sure,' she said at last. 'I think…'

'Yes?'

'I think I'm still quite little. But I seem to have been little for a very long time.' She studied Allie intently. 'Why are you here?' she asked.

A very good question, Allie thought.

'I, well, I met your brother,' she said. 'And…'

But Babette was shaking her head. 'Haven't got a brother,' she said.

'I think you have. Nick?'

Babette scowled. 'Don't know anyone called Nick,' she said.

'You must do! He lives right here in this house. He told me he's sometimes called Donald?'

Again, a blank look and a shake of the head.

'You said your mother is Julia, right? And Julia has a son, so–'

'That's not so!' insisted Babette. 'My mother only has me. And she says that my daddy only gave me to her because she wanted something to love.'

'Your daddy?' Allie was getting more confused by the moment. 'Well then, what's he called?'

'Mahoun,' said Babette.

Allie frowned. 'That's an odd name,' she said.

'It's what my mother calls him,' insisted Babette.

Allie was beginning to tire of asking so many questions. 'Well, look, it's very late, Babette, so perhaps you should try and get some sleep,' she suggested. 'We both should.'

Babette looked disappointed. 'I usually have a story before I go to sleep,' she said. 'Can you tell me one?'

'A story?' Allie looked at the girl doubtfully. 'Do you have a book I can read from?'

Babette shook her head. 'Mummy always makes up the stories,' she said.

'I see. Well, er… let me think. I'm not sure I'm any good at making things up. What stories do I know?' Allie cast around in her head, trying to remember the fairy tales she had liked when she was little. 'How about the Elves and the Shoemaker?' she suggested.

Babette shook her head. 'I've heard that one,' she said. 'It's boring.'

'Okay. Well, what about…?'

'Make up a story!' suggested Babette. 'Go on. That's what my mummy does. She makes them up out of nothing.' She leaned closer as if to confide a secret. 'Sometimes she puts me in them.'

'I… don't know if I can do that.'

'Course you can! Made up stories are the best.'

Allie didn't feel entirely convinced by the argument but thought that she'd have to at least attempt what Babette was suggesting if she was ever going to get back to sleep. 'All right then,' she said. 'Let me see. There once was a little girl called Babette.'

Babette smiled delightedly. She cuddled Molly closer. 'Do you hear that, Molly? Another one about me!' She gazed up at Allie. 'Go on,' she prompted.

Encouraged, Allie began to improvise. 'Erm… Babette was a good little girl, but she had a doll called Molly and Molly wasn't good at all, in fact, she could be very naughty…'

'Are you listening, Molly?' murmured Babette. 'This is also about you.'

'One day, Babette's mummy gave her a kitten to play with…'

Allie continued to tell the story, aware as she did so of Babette's surprisingly powerful little arm curled around her like a band of ice. Oddly, after a short while, Allie could hear her own voice speaking, but it seemed to her that it was coming across a great distance – and while at first she only pictured the images that accompanied the story in her mind's eye, as the tale progressed, it was as though she was observing them as the action unfolded;

as though she had chanced upon it and could only watch, like a helpless bystander, as the events played out in front of her.

'Babette loved the kitten very much... and she would spend hours playing with it...'

Now Allie was standing in the corner of the room, watching as Babette dangled a length of bright green wool in front of a tiny ginger kitten, which was reaching up with its front paws to pat at the swaying strand. On the bed, propped against a heap of pillows, Molly watched Babette and the kitten as they played – and it seemed to Allie that she could detect a hint of malice in the doll's blank green eyes... as though she really was watching.

'After a while, Babette grew tired and soon she fell fast asleep–'

Sure enough, there was Babette, stretching herself out on her bed, her eyes closing, her breath becoming slower. The kitten lay down alongside her, its flank pressed against Babette for warmth and, very soon, it too closed its eyes. Now it was night-time and somewhere an old clock ticked laboriously through the minutes. Allie watched and continued to tell the story.

'When Babette was in a deep sleep, Molly began to stir...'

And Allie wished now she could stop telling the story, because, sure enough, there was movement in the doll's body – the little arms pushing down on the mattress, the legs bending, then straightening to bring the short, dumpy body upright. And the face, that pale china face was suddenly soft, animated, the smile widening as the eyes fixed on the sleeping kitten. The red lips curved back, displaying tiny white pegs of teeth. Molly began to move closer, across the bedcovers, her pudgy arms outstretched, and the kitten slept on, unaware as Molly came nearer, as her malleable fingers with their shiny red nails reached out to grip the kitten by the throat.

'Wake up, Allie.' Her own voice, urging her to come back to reality, but somehow she was unable to make herself obey; she had to keep watching as the doll's hands fastened on the kitten with incredible power and began to rend and tear. The kitten woke suddenly, yowling in pain and fear but it was already too late. A dark red spray spattered the white bed covers.

'Wake up, Allie, wake up, please wake up!'

But still the dream had her in its grip as surely as Molly had the kitten, squeezing, tearing, snuffing out its brief existence. It was only a tiny creature, but the noise it made as it died was immense, loud enough to wake Babette who added her own screams to the tumult, a sound that seemed to rise in a wave and engulf Allie, until it felt as though her head was about to explode...

Only then did she wake to find that the first rays of sun were breaking through a small gap in the curtains. She glanced frantically around. She was alone in the bed. There was no sign of Babette, no indication that she had ever been there. A dream, Allie decided. Had to be. She shook her head, banishing the last waves of sleep and then she threw back the covers, dressed herself quickly and made her way downstairs.

6

SIGNING UP

She found Nick exactly where she had left him, sitting at the big table in the dining room. As she came in, he was taking something from a small silver platter, something small that he lifted to his mouth with a thumb and forefinger and crunched between his teeth. A raisin, perhaps? A black grape? He glanced up as she came in. 'Ah, good morning!' he said, replacing the lid of the salver and pushing it to one side. She saw that he had been going through a thick sheaf of papers, all of which had been laboriously scrawled on, line after line of closely packed characters, hand-written in black ink. He gave her a dazzling smile, his blue eyes burning into hers. 'I trust you slept well,' he said.

She shook her head. 'Not really. I had a dream. At least, I think it was a dream. There was a wee girl. Babette?'

Nick made a small tutting sound, then shrugged his shoulders. 'Young children can be an annoyance,' he said. 'But sometimes they are a necessity.'

Allie stared at him. 'She's real then?' she murmured.

'I'm afraid so.' He seemed to dismiss the subject and waved a hand at the heavily laden table. 'Sit down and have some breakfast,' he suggested. 'Then you'll feel better. Tell me, are you a tea or a coffee person?'

'Coffee,' she said. She looked doubtfully at the array of silver salvers in front of her, which as far as she could tell had not been changed from the previous night. But when she lifted the lid of the nearest of them, she found it was heaped with crispy fried bacon. Nick, meanwhile, had lifted a silver coffee pot and was filling two elegant china cups with steaming black liquid. He indicated a jug of milk standing nearby. 'Help yourself to that if you want it,' he said. 'I prefer my coffee au naturel.'

Allie was in the act of lifting another lid. She'd been hoping for scrambled eggs and she wasn't disappointed. 'How do you do it?' she asked, exasperated.

'Do what?' he asked her, sounding genuinely puzzled.

'Have everything ready like this. I mean, you couldn't have known I was going to arrive just now.'

'Of course I could,' he assured her. 'You're my guest. It's my job to know when you're going to arrive. And what kind of a manager would I be if I couldn't make my new client happy?' He lifted his cup to his mouth and took a sip, then smacked his lips loudly. 'Perfect,' he said.

She added milk and sugar to her own cup and had a sip. She was more used to instant coffee, but this tasted fresh and strong, cutting through her sleep-addled senses like a knife. 'Have you even been to bed?' she asked him.

He shook his head. 'Far too much to do,' he said. 'Busy, busy, busy! I had to get the contract written, didn't I?' He made a theatrical flourish over the heap of paper. 'And here it is, all ready for you to sign.'

Allie paused in the act of buttering a hunk of wholemeal bread. 'What's in it?' she asked suspiciously.

He slid the pages across the table to her. 'Have a read,' he said. 'If there's anything you don't like, just let me know. It's not too late to amend things.'

'It looks like there's an awful lot here to take in,' she said doubtfully.

He shrugged. 'There's no hurry. In your own time.'

Allie sighed. She took a couple of strips of bacon and laid them onto the slice of buttered bread, then folded it over to make a sandwich. She took a generous bite, chewed for a few moments, then turned the pages around so that she could look at the cover. She saw that it was dated in the top left hand corner and that there was a title, written in fancy old-fashioned calligraphy, the letters featuring elaborate flourishes and curlicues. She read the title to herself.

A Contract between, on the one hand, Miss Allie Lawrence and, on the other, Mr Nick Mahoun.

Mahoun. Wasn't that the name that Babette had used when speaking of her father? So it had been a surname, not a first name. But why had the little girl said that she didn't have a brother? It didn't make any sense. And besides, that had only been a dream, hadn't it?

Allie turned over the top page, to find that the next was thick with words, hundreds of them, so closely crammed together, they were virtually bleeding into each other. It made them really difficult to read.

This is to certify that I, Allie Lawrence, of 34, Welton Avenue, Killiecrankie, Perthshire, do hereby certify that I have willingly and of my own accord signed this document, and that I agree to abide by the stipulations made by Mr Nick Mahoun of Mahoun Enterprises Incorporated, that in exchange for his guidance and advice in the furtheration of my career as an actor, I shall undertake to give him full co-operation at all times and will endeavour to fulfil all obligations that should present themselves in the continuation of the various tasks...'

It went on like this for page after page, until the words became ever more unfathomable and swam in front of Allie's eyes like a swarm of vividly-coloured tropical fish. After a while, she had to stop reading.

'This is very hard to follow,' she told Nick. 'I'm not sure I understand even half of it. Don't you have a computer printout or something?

He looked affronted by the suggestion. 'This is how I always put together my contracts,' he said. 'I don't much care for computers.'

'Julia told me you wanted to move with the times,' protested Allie.

'Some things can't be changed,' he told her.

'Well that's a shame, because I can hardly make head nor tail of this.'

He shook his head. 'That's legal speak for you,' he said. 'It's a curse. But don't worry, I can translate anything you're not sure of into simple, everyday language.' He reached out and turned to the back page. 'I just require your signature here,' he said, pointing. 'And I can explain anything you've a problem with on the way.'

'On the way?' she echoed.

'To Edinburgh,' he said. 'Well, we mustn't waste any more time. We need to strike while the iron is hot. You're familiar with that expression, I suppose? We need to get you sorted. Accommodation, clothes, contacts...'

'Er... yes, sure, but... well, I really don't think I should sign something that I haven't read properly. What if I'm letting myself in for... trouble?'

He pulled a face, as though he'd just got a bad taste in his mouth. 'What do you mean?' he asked. 'Trouble?'

'Well, it's just, what if signing this means I'm liable to pay a lot of money that I don't have? My dad always says...'

'Oh, so your father is an expert in the world of theatre, is he?'

'No, I didn't say that!'

'Your father is a lawyer, perhaps, or a solicitor?'

'Well, no, but...'

'Do you mind if I ask you what he does for a living?'

'He... well, if you must know, he sells insurance.'

'Ah ha!' Nick nodded as though he'd suspected it all along. 'Now why does that not surprise me?' he murmured. 'Those people pedalling their empty promises and then wriggling out of them at the first opportunity! Oh, we'd all take their word for something, wouldn't we? Those people are crooks, Allie. Nothing more, nothing less.'

She felt a pang of displeasure at this. After all, he was talking about her dad, the man who drove her to school most mornings, who made her a mug of hot chocolate every night before she went to bed. She was about to comment, but Nick was looking across the table at her and his blue eyes seemed to shimmer with such intensity that she felt her hostility start to evaporate. 'It's just that... well, I don't want to be a mug here,' she said. 'A pushover.'

'Let me assure you,' he murmured. 'Money is of no interest to me. It is irrelevant. I neither seek nor value it. I can absolutely promise you that if you sign this...' He reached out an index finger to tap the pages in front of her. '... you will owe me not one penny. In fact, I would be insulted if you offered me money in exchange for my services.'

Allie felt baffled. 'Then, what? I mean, what's in it for you?'

Nick smiled. 'Old-fashioned things,' he said. 'The satisfaction that comes from a job well done. The delight of introducing a new talent to the world. The simple joy of helping somebody to achieve her dearest ambition. Does that not count for anything these days?'

'But there must be something else you want from me!' she protested. 'Nobody does anything for anybody unless there's something in it for them. I'm sorry, but I really believe that.' She took a deep breath. She had to say what was on her mind, even if it made her feel very uncomfortable. 'Is it... are you expecting to...?' She raised her eyebrows suggestively. 'You know.'

He stared at her, looking completely baffled. 'I know what?'

'Is it that you want a bit of...?'

He shook his head. 'I haven't the faintest idea what you're talking about.'

'I mean... were you expecting some kind of... sex thing? With me?'

Now he looked absolutely horrified and she couldn't help feeling weirdly disappointed.

'What on earth gave you that idea?' he protested. 'Have I said anything that would suggest it?'

'Well, yes, you have, if you want to know the truth. All that stuff about me being so talented and everything? It's the kind of thing that men say to get you into bed. You could be just trying it on!'

Nick became suddenly rather agitated. 'Perhaps I've misjudged you,' he said. 'I thought you were intelligent, but perhaps you're just a silly girl who isn't ready for what I can offer.' He snatched up the papers. 'I sat up the whole night drafting this, but no matter. If it doesn't meet with your approval, let's just get rid of it, shall we? I wouldn't want you to do something you're not entirely comfortable with.' He stood up from the table and went over to the fireplace, where Allie could see that a fire was burning in the hearth. He leaned forward as if to throw the papers into the flames.

'NO!' Allie was suddenly on her feet, aware that all her hopes and aspirations were about to go up in smoke. She pictured herself knocking on the door of her parents' house; she saw her mother's triumphant smile as Allie stepped through the doorway with her tail between her legs. 'No, wait! Please, just give me a minute! I need to think about this.'

'You've had plenty of time to think, Allie. You've had the whole damned night! You've clearly already made up your mind about me. I think I should start again, look for somebody more trusting, more deserving of what I have to offer.' His hand moved closer to the fire. 'Let's just call it quits, shall we?'

'No, please, bring it back. I'll do it. I'll sign it!'

He hesitated, turned to look at her. 'You're sure?' he said quietly. 'Because you know, it's no skin off my nose, either way.'

'Yes, yes, please. I'm sorry, I didn't mean to…'

'You do understand, it's pointless if I do not have your full co-operation.'

'You have it,' she assured him. 'Please, come back to the table.'

He frowned and seemed to ponder the matter for a little while longer before he turned and walked slowly back to his chair. 'If you insist,' he said.

'I do. As long as you promise you won't be asking for money. You said something before about… the usual agency fee?'

He smirked. 'A mere turn of phrase,' he said. 'All I want from you, Allie, is your commitment. All I ask is that you give me everything that's in there.' And he pointed a finger at her chest. 'Your heart and soul is all I require.'

'Promise?'

'Most solemnly.'

She nodded, reassured. 'OK then,' she murmured.

He slid the papers back across the table to her and opened them to the final page, where he indicated a dotted line. 'Sign here,' he said, his voice as smooth as warm honey.

'I don't have a…'

The pen seemed to sprout magically from his fingers, a chunky marbled fountain pen. He handed it to her. 'You're doing the right thing,' he whispered. He placed a hand on her shoulder and once again, she felt that familiar warmth flood through her, making her tingle. 'You won't regret this.'

'I hope not,' she said quietly. She uncapped the pen.

He turned away and studied the fireplace. 'When you are up on the stage, basking in the applause of hundreds of people,' he said, 'I shall remind you of this moment, of the doubts you had. And the two of us will laugh about it together.'

She nodded. An idea came to her. She leaned forward and signed on the dotted line.

'There,' he said, turning back and he was smiling now, an angelic smile that seemed to light up his entire face, reminding her of how handsome he was. 'We have a deal,' he said. He swept the sheaf of papers up from the table, rolled them into a cylinder and slipped them into one of the pockets of his long coat. 'Now, I have a few last preparations to make,' he said, standing up from the table. 'You stay here and finish your breakfast. I'll inform Tam we'll be ready to leave in half an hour.' He studied her for a moment, then turned away and walked out of the room.

She went back to her sandwich and took an exploratory bite, but it seemed to have lost most of its flavour. She scanned the table for something else and her eye fell on the small salver that Nick had been eating from when she first came in. Intrigued, she reached across the table and pulled it closer, thinking perhaps that there was something in there that might rekindle her appetite. As she moved it closer she was aware of a dull vibration coming from within the dish. Puzzled, she lifted the lid and looked at the contents.

The salver was full of bluebottles. They were moving sluggishly around on the silver plate and she wondered why they didn't just fly away. But then she looked closer and realised that the wings of each insect had been carefully removed. She made a small sound of disgust and dropped the lid back into position, then pushed the salver back to the other side of the table.

Her gorge rose and for a moment she thought she was going to be sick, but somehow she managed to get the impulse under control. She leaned back in her seat and took a gulp of coffee. One thing was for sure.

She had completely lost her appetite.

7

DRIVE TIME

The limousine cruised smoothly along a country road and Allie found herself once again sitting face-to-face with Nick. He was beguilingly handsome, she thought, his skin flawless, his blue eyes fathomless. He was studying that little leatherbound book again, as though something in its pages held him absolutely spellbound and as the car covered mile after mile, Allie found herself wishing that Tam would put on the radio or something; but of course, when she looked through the glass and over his shoulder, she could see that the car's walnut dashboard boasted neither radio nor CD player. Which seemed to be par for the course with Nick. She sighed and decided that in the absence of music, she would try and strike up some conversation.

'So, where exactly are we headed?' she asked.

He lifted his gaze from the pages of his notebook and studied her quizzically for a moment. He seemed slightly irked by the question.

'We're going to Edinburgh,' he said. 'I must have told you five times.'

'Well, yes, I know that, but, where's our first port of call?'

He closed the notebook with a sigh and slipped it into the pocket of his long coat. 'Our number one priority is to find you somewhere to live,' he said.

'I see. And have you any idea where that might be?'

He shrugged as though it was of little importance. 'Obviously, we'll need to find the right place. Something suitable for a young lady living alone.'

Allie smiled involuntarily at his old-fashioned phrasing.

'What's funny?' he asked her, tilting his head to the side once again, as though entranced.

'Oh, I was just wondering what my mother would say if she heard you.'

'Ah. There's a thought. Your parents. We'll need to get them on board.'

Allie didn't much like the sound of that. 'What do you mean?' she asked. 'Get them on board, how?'

'We'll need to reassure them that I have your best interests at heart.'

'And how do you propose to do that, exactly?'

'Well, I'll meet with them at my earliest opportunity and explain the situation.'

Allie smiled ruefully. 'Good luck with that,' she said.

'I take it you don't really get along with your parents?'

'They... I suppose they mean well. But they don't seem to realise I'm sixteen now and I need space to do my own thing. They always want to keep me at home, all to themselves, their wee girl.' The subject made her think about the strange little visitor she'd had the previous night. 'Babette,' she murmured. 'What's her story?'

He seemed amused by her question. 'There's no story,' he said. 'She's just Julia's daughter.'

'Yes, but, who's her father? I did ask and she said it was somebody called...'

'Babette's father was a bad person,' interrupted Nick. 'A totally unsuitable parent. I thought it best to remove her from his influence. And Julia wanted something to care about, something to lavish her attention on. I thought Babette would suit her down to the ground.' He waved a hand as though dismissing the subject. 'It was all a very long time ago,' he said.

'Can't have been that long,' argued Allie. 'Babette's what? Six or seven years old? And you would have been twelve or thirteen, so–'

'Looks can be deceptive,' said Nick, mysteriously. 'And sometimes we want to keep things at their best, don't we?'

'How do you mean?'

'Well, flowers are best plucked young, before the autumn withers them. Fruit tastes its finest when it has just begun to approach maturity. It's only fine wines and cheeses that improve with age.' He turned his head to peer out of the window. Verdant hedgerows sped past in a blur of green and the sky above them was a serene blue, dotted here and there with little wisps of white cirrus. 'I told Tam to take the country roads,' said Nick. 'I despise motorways. All those stupid people, so intent on getting to their destinations in the shortest possible space of time.' He snorted. 'They should relish the opportunity to travel at a more sedate pace.'

Allie shook her head. 'You don't talk like anyone I've ever met,' she told him. 'Were you home-schooled?'

'Schooled?' He looked puzzled. 'I wasn't schooled at all.'

Allie shook her head. 'You must have been. Everyone has to be schooled. It's the law, isn't it?'

He shrugged. 'I wouldn't know about that. I don't much care for laws. I'm a great believer in instinct, in following what you feel in your gut. That's how I've always operated. Why would I follow the example of somebody else?'

'Well, you weren't joking when you said you needed to move into the twenty-first century.'

'Who told you I said that?' he asked her.

'Julia. She said you were worried about coming across as old-fashioned. And the fact is, you do. Big time.'

'How should I speak?' he asked her and his expression looked deadly serious. 'Teach me some phrases.'

'Seriously?'

'Of course.'

'Well…' Now she felt awkward. Most of the time, she didn't really know what people were talking about at all. 'I really wouldn't know where to start,' she admitted.

'You must surely have some advice for me?'

'Well, you could be a little less… formal.'

'Formal? How am I formal?

'Er, never mind.' Allie made a quick attempt to change the subject. 'Can I ask you something?'

'Of course you may!'

'You know at breakfast this morning?'

He nodded.

'Those things you were eating—' She tried not to let the revulsion show on her face. 'What was that all about?'

'Protein,' he said. 'I don't really go in for big meals, as I'm sure you've noticed. Digestive problems. But I like to keep my energy levels up. I find those little fellows very nutritious and quite flavoursome. Tam collects them for me and removes the wings, so they can't fly away.' He reached into his pocket and pulled out a small buzzing metal box. 'I always carry some with me, because you never know when you might need an energy boost. I don't suppose…?' He held the box out to her but she shook her head with a grimace.

'I couldn't,' she said.

'I'm sure you could,' he told her. 'In the right circumstances. People are often amazed to discover what they're capable of when push comes to shove. But I completely understand.' He slipped the box back into his pocket. 'Do let me know if you change your mind.'

'I will. Er, so, look – when we find somewhere for me to live – how exactly am I going to pay for it?'

He looked annoyed at the question. 'Allie, I have already told you. Don't worry about the money. It's of no importance. I will take care of the little details.'

'Yes, but it's not a little detail, is it? How you pay for things, that's really important.'

She broke off with a gasp of alarm as there was a sudden screech of brakes, followed by a powerful impact that shook Allie in her seat. The car lurched to an abrupt stop. Up ahead of them, Tam said something under his breath that sounded distinctly like a curse.

'What's happened?' demanded Nick.

'We hit something,' snarled Tam, and Allie thought to herself that these were the first words she had ever heard the big man say. He had a deep, gravelly voice with what sounded like a Glaswegian accent. He opened the driver's door and went to stand at the front of the car. He stood there, hands on his hips, looking down at something that Allie couldn't see.

'Let's have a closer look,' muttered Nick. He opened his door and got out. Allie followed him and they walked around to join Tam. Allie lifted a hand to her mouth, smothering an involuntary cry. A young deer was stretched out on the tarmac, just in front of the car's crumpled hood. Its eyes were wide open and its reddish brown flank was rising and falling rapidly, as it struggled to breathe. Allie could see a vivid splash of blood across its chest and she couldn't help but notice that one of its skinny front legs was broken and splayed at an impossible angle, a white splinter of bone protruding through the caramel coloured flesh. She felt her stomach lurch and had to avert her gaze.

'Damned thing jumped right out in front of me,' muttered Tam. 'Didn't have time to stop.'

'It's all right,' said Nick. 'Accidents will happen.' He stepped closer and crouched down beside the deer, as if to examine it more closely. 'It's only a fawn,' he said. 'Can't be more than a few months old.'

Allie became aware of a movement in the hedgerow to her left and turning, she saw a fully grown deer standing in the dappled shadows, looking fearfully back at the road. Allie realised it must be the mother. She must have been leading the fawn across the road and had narrowly missed being struck by the car herself. Allie was about to say something but the words died in her throat as Nick reached out his hands as if to embrace the stricken fawn. He placed his left hand gently on its chest and his right onto its shattered leg. He began to slide the right hand gently up and down the leg, as though soothing it and weirdly, miraculously, as Allie watched, the broken limb began to straighten.

The fawn's eyes bulged in terror and its chest rose and fell at a frantic pace. Now Nick was murmuring something under his breath, words that Allie couldn't quite catch, but whatever he was saying sounded gentle and reassuring. The leg straightened even more, the ragged wound seemed to heal and, as Allie continued to stare in mute disbelief, the fawn struggled upright, took a couple of uncertain steps and then trotted quickly across the road to join its mother. The two creatures moved off together, pushing through the hedgerow and into the field beyond. Allie caught a glimpse of them running off through long grass, the fawn now appearing to move easily and naturally. Nick stood up and watched them for a moment. Then he turned and started to move back towards the open rear door of the car.

But Allie barred his way. 'What?' she cried. 'What just happened?'

'I think you saw what happened,' said Nick smoothly.

'Yes, but its leg was broken!' she protested.

He nodded. 'So it would appear,' he agreed. 'But it seems fine now.' He winked, stepped past her and strolled back to the open door. 'We should press on, Tam,' he said over his shoulder. 'Time's moving on.'

'Aye, sir.' Tam turned to walk back around the car and as he did so he caught Allie's eye and looked straight at her. He didn't say anything but his expression seemed to suggest that he understood her amazement, and yes, it was incredible, but he was well used to this kind of thing. As he moved past the front of the car, Allie noticed another detail. The bonnet, which had been so badly crumpled only a few moments before, now looked perfectly normal.

'No freakin' way,' she whispered under her breath.

'Come along, Allie,' said Nick's voice from the car. 'We need to get going.'

She stood for a moment, thinking over what she'd seen. Her rational mind tried to come up with possible explanations for it. The fawn's leg hadn't really been broken. The bonnet hadn't really been damaged. But she knew that she had seen what she had seen and, whatever else happened, she couldn't now unsee it. She turned, walked numbly back to the open rear door, and climbed into her seat. She slammed the door shut and sat there looking at Nick. He gazed right back at her, his face expressionless.

'Drive on, Tam,' he said. And the car moved slowly away.

8

LUXURIOUSLY APPOINTED

Almost before Allie knew it the car had made the Queensferry Crossing and was entering the outskirts of Edinburgh. She would normally have been very excited – especially when she saw the castle, perched up on the hill away to her right, looking like something from a fairy story. But she couldn't think straight because her head kept filling with the image of the fawn's shattered leg as it had mended, straightened, healed itself under the soothing touch of Nick's hands. She couldn't begin to understand what had happened back there but she knew that it frightened her.

The car was cruising sedately along Queen Street now and Nick seemed to be studying a row of shops on the far side of the road as though looking for something in particular. 'Here,' he said suddenly, and Tam brought the vehicle to an abrupt halt, instigating an indignant blare of car horns from behind him, but he took no notice of them.

'We can't park here,' said Allie, trying to be helpful and pointing to a sign on the pavement. Sure enough, a traffic warden in a brightly-coloured yellow jacket and peaked cap had spotted them and was hurrying over, reaching into a leather wallet on his belt as he did so. As he came up to the car, Nick wound the rear window down. The warden saw him and leaned down, shaking his head.

He started to speak in an officious voice. 'I'm sorry, sir, I'm afraid you're not allowed to…'

'Go away,' said Nick, calmly.

The man's face registered puzzlement then suddenly turned blank.

'Yes, sir,' he said, meekly.

He turned on his heel and wandered off along the pavement, looking dazed. Allie stared after him in amazement. From what her father had told her about such people, they didn't usually make allowances for those who parked in the wrong spot.

Nick muttered something under his breath and the traffic warden turned sharp right, and stepped into the road out of Allie's line of sight. There was a screech of brakes and the sound of a sudden impact and suddenly people on the pavement were running past the car to go and view the damage.

Nick ignored the commotion. He threw open the door of the limousine and climbed out, snatching up his cane as he went. Allie started to follow him, but he made a dismissive gesture with one hand. 'Wait in the car,' he told her.

She was about to object but the expression on his face suggested that he wasn't interested in discussing the point, so she shrugged and sank back into her seat as he slammed the door shut. She watched as Nick crossed the road and went in through the swing door of McNight Francis, a rather grand-looking estate agent with a series of opulent properties displayed on illuminated screens in the windows. Allie saw him go straight to a female receptionist sitting at a desk. He said something to her and she nodded, gazing up at him as though intrigued. Moments later, a young man in a stylish grey suit came out of an inner office and spoke to Nick, smiling as he did so. He was good-looking but, Allie noted, nowhere near as handsome as Nick. The two of them chatted for a moment and then the young man turned and led Nick into an office, closing the door behind them.

Allie sighed, turned her head to study Tam's enormous shoulders.

'Who is he?' she asked.

There was a long silence before Tam half-turned in his seat and gave her an impassive look. 'What kind of question is that?' he muttered.

'I'm not sure,' she admitted. 'But I'm really confused. The thing he did with the deer. You saw that leg. It was broken like a stick. He touched it and it… it mended.'

Tam gave a slow shrug. 'Aye,' he said. 'I suppose it did.'

'You suppose?' Allie glared at him. 'You did see it, didn't you?'

He sighed, nodded. 'Aye,' he said. 'I saw it.'

'So, what does it mean? What does it make him? You looked like it meant nothing to you.'

'You haven't witnessed what I have,' said Tam, matter-of-factly. 'That was nothing. I've seen him lift a mountain and throw it into the sun.' His dead eyes studied her to see what she made of the remark. 'When you've seen that, girl, then come back and ask me silly questions.' And with that, he turned away to study the road ahead.

'This is nuts,' said Allie, to nobody in particular. 'This is bonkers.' On impulse, she reached out and grabbed the handle of the door, meaning to pull it open. She realised with a sinking feeling that it was locked. 'Tam,' she said quietly. 'Open the door please. I want to get out.'

He didn't turn his head. 'He said to wait in the car.'

'I don't care what he said. I want to get out.'

There was a long silence then. 'If you don't open

the door, I'll scream,' she warned him. 'I'll scream till somebody comes.'

He finally turned his head again and now he looked vaguely amused by what she'd said. 'Scream away,' he suggested. 'Nobody will come. Nobody will even hear you. And if they do hear you, none of them will want to get involved. That's how they are.' He seemed to think for a moment. 'Besides, you don't even want to get out of the car.'

'What makes you say that?' she protested.

'Because nobody ever does. They always want to know more.'

She glared at him. 'Are you saying that there have been others? Others like me?'

He nodded. 'Aye,' he said. 'There have been… thousands of them, I suppose. All kinds of people. All different ages. And not one of them ever chose to get out of the car. Not one.' His lips curved into a strange grin, revealing his misshapen yellow teeth. 'But I don't know, maybe you're different. Let's see, shall we?' There was a sudden dull thunk as the door unlocked itself. 'Go on, then,' said Tam. 'Away ye go, if that's what you really want.'

Allie licked her lips. She reached out to touch the door handle and was momentarily shocked at how cold it felt on this bright summer's day, like an icicle against her fingers. She took a deep breath.

'Go on,' said Tam. 'I'll not stop ye.'

'What will you say to him?' Allie asked him. 'What will you say if he comes back and I'm not here?'

'I'll tell him you had a change of heart.'

'And he won't be angry with you?'

Another shrug of those huge shoulders. 'Maybe. Maybe not. He's been angry with me before.' He shook his head.

'But it makes no difference, because you aren't going to do it, are ye? If you were, you'd be gone by now.'

'Maybe... maybe I'm just thinking it through,' Allie told him.

'Aye. And maybe you're thinking, "What else can he do? What else is he capable of? And most importantly, what could he give me?" And when there are thoughts like that in your head, why, then it's really very hard to leave, isn't it? The thought that you might miss some more wonders.' He chuckled unpleasantly. 'You see, ye are all the same in the end. Curiosity always gets the better of ye.' He lifted his head as the door of the estate agent opened and Nick and the young man came out. 'Last chance,' he whispered. 'It's now or never...'

But Allie had already released her grip on the handle. Tam was absolutely correct, she decided. She couldn't leave now, not after what she'd already seen.

The car door opened and Nick climbed in. He slid into his customary seat. An instant later, the other man followed him and took a place beside Allie. He was handsome in a well-groomed sort of way, his blonde hair immaculately cut, his suit pressed to within an inch of its life. He smelled of a musky cologne and had, Allie thought, a slightly dazed expression on his chiselled features, much like the one the traffic warden had displayed a few minutes earlier. The young man placed a leather briefcase on the seat beside him and then reached out and pulled the door shut.

'This is Marco,' said Nick brightly. 'We've just had a wee chat and he thinks he has the perfect place for us. Drive on, Tam. Marco will give you directions as we go.'

Tam nodded and the car moved slowly away from the curb, accompanied once again by the sounds of blaring car horns from just behind them. As they moved on they passed an agitated cluster of people in the road, standing around something lying on the tarmac. Allie caught a glimpse of a neon yellow jacket splashed with crimson and turned her head away.

'What happened there?' asked Marco, dreamily.

'People need to pay proper attention when they're crossing the road,' said Nick dismissively.

Marco nodded. 'Nice motor,' he observed. Despite his European name, he had what sounded to Allie like an Essex accent. He stroked the leather upholstery of his armrest with one hand. 'I won't ask you what you paid for it.' He chuckled. 'Makes my VW Golf look pretty pale by comparison.'

'The car's been in my family for a long time,' said Nick. 'It's rather old-fashioned but it suits me.' He gestured to Allie. 'This is the young lady I was telling you about.'

'Oh, right. Cool.' Marco took Allie's hand and shook it vigorously. She tried not to wince at the power in his fingers. This was clearly a young man who worked out on a daily basis. 'Nick tells me you're gonna be a big star.'

Allie didn't know what to say to that. She just smiled vacantly.

'Now, the place I've got in mind for you, Allie… you don't mind if I call you that, do you?'

'Er, no, not at all.'

'It's on the Quartermile. I expect you've heard of it?'

'Er, sure!' She hadn't, but didn't want to appear ignorant.

'It's a relatively new development, there's still a bit of work going on there, but I think it will be absolutely perfect for somebody like yourself, a creative person.' He lifted his head to look through the glass at Tam. 'Take the next right,' he said. .' He turned back, smiled. 'I'd love a place there myself but I can't afford it.'

Allie looked at Nick, alarmed by this, but his expression didn't falter. He was smiling confidently.

'Tell Allie about the amenities,' he suggested.

'Oh, sure. Well, there's a service charge…'

'Naturally,' said Nick.

'… but that comes with a lot of extras. You get membership at the local Pure Gym, access to bike storage in the basement and there's even a laundry area with state-of-the-art washer-driers. Now, I'm going to be honest with you, Allie, this isn't the biggest apartment you'll ever see, not by a long shot, but for somebody on their own, it's a brilliant option and of course, you'll be in the heart of the city. You'll be minutes away from the best bars, nightclubs, cinemas… oh and of course, the theatres, that's sure to be a must for you, am I right?'

'Cool,' said Nick and Marco gave him an odd look.

'There's underground parking too, you'll be needing that, I suppose.' He lifted his gaze again again. 'Hang a left here,' he instructed Tam. He turned back to look at Allie. 'So… are you working on something right now?' he asked her.

'I, er… how do you mean?' she muttered.

'I mean, what's your next role?'

'Oh, er… well, I…'

'Marco, Allie prefers to keep things like that under wraps,' Nick told him. 'Rest assured it's something big – but we wouldn't want it to get out before we're ready to go public. I'm sure you understand.'

'Oh, absolutely. Yeah, no worries, I totally appreciate where you're coming from with that.' Marco looked up. 'Here's our turning,' he announced. 'Drive straight up and go around the side of the block on your right, ' he told Tam. He turned back to Allie. 'Don't let all the building work put you off,' he warned her. 'It's busy right now, but once this is finished it's going to be one of the most desirable addresses in the city.'

He was right about the industry, Allie thought. They were moving into an area where tall glass buildings reared up on every side of them – but around these constructions moved battalions of workmen in fluorescent yellow jackets and hard hats. Huge brightly-coloured machines were digging up the ground or flattening it back down again. The long metallic arms of cherry-pickers moved bunches of workmen up and down the face of a building, so they could clean the glass or install new panes or attach blocks of grey cladding. Engines rumbled, road drills rattled and electronic alarms beeped repetitively as if to ensure that nobody would ever be in danger of missing their presence. Allie was put in mind of an ants' nest she'd accidentally trodden on during a country walk when she was little, the furious little creatures streaming backwards and forwards as they raced to mend the damage that she'd done to their home.

'It's much quieter where we're going,' Marco assured her. He gave Tam a last instruction. 'Carry on to the end of the street, hang a right and you'll find parking spaces up at the top,' he said.

Happily, he hadn't been lying about the noise. As the car turned around the side of a tower block, the hustle and bustle receded dramatically. 'It'll all be like this eventually,' Marco assured them. The building they were approaching sat amidst carefully tended lawns. Unlike the gleaming glass boxes they had passed earlier, it was a fortress-like four-storey building of grey stone, replete with huge windows and wide balconies. 'These are the old hospital buildings,' Marco explained. 'Some of the best flat conversions ever.' Tam eased the limo into an empty spot and Marco opened the door and climbed out. He waited politely as Allie got out and then turned back to help Nick.

'This way,' said Marco and they followed him across a stone-flagged entrance to a set of glass doors. He punched a four-digit code into a keypad beside the door and pushed it open.

'Fabulous security here,' he said quietly, and led them across a marble tiled lobby to the lift. 'Second to none.' He pressed a button and the stainless steel doors swished silently open. 'Now, Allie, the place I have in mind for you is up on the first floor,' said Marco. 'It's only just come back onto the market. The previous tenants moved to Dubai.'

They stepped into the lift and waited for the doors to slide shut. 'I don't mind telling you that this is my personal favourite out of all the properties we have on our books,' said Marco, lowering his voice as if sharing a secret. 'Wait until you see the view!'

To Allie, everything seemed to be drifting by in a dream. She vaguely registered stepping out of the lift again and crossing the hall to a doorway, which Marco opened with an electronic key. And then they were inside the place and she was staring around in open-mouthed astonishment because everything looked so clean, so fresh, so cool. They stepped first into a decent-sized open plan living room. It had solid wood flooring, white painted walls, and stylish black leather sofas. One wall consisted of a long run of floor-to-ceiling glass doors, which looked out onto a balcony. Beyond it, Allie could see a stretch of meticulously tended grass which led to ornate metal railings; and beyond that was a great stretch of grass, dotted with trees and bisected by paths along which people walked and jogged and cycled. Marco slid back a door and they stepped out onto the balcony and stood there, gazing down like monarchs contemplating their kingdom. The scent of new-mown grass filled Allie's nostrils.

'This is the Meadows,' said Marco matter-of-factly. 'We like to boast that when you live here, your back garden is the finest park in Edinburgh.' He gestured to the ranks of people picnicking on the grass. 'Don't worry,' he said. 'They can't get in. But you can use that space whenever you feel like it. I don't know if you're into fitness, but you can jog, cycle, and like I said, the gym is just a short walk from here.'

Marco went back inside, still talking, and Nick went after him, but Allie hesitated, reluctant to tear her gaze from the gorgeous view laid out below her. She couldn't believe this was happening. For a moment she had a powerful conviction that she was still home in her parent's house in her dowdy little bedroom, that she was asleep and dreaming this. But, she told herself, if it was a dream, it was the most intense, vivid one that she'd ever experienced. She couldn't remember when she had last felt so happy. The green swathes of the Meadows blurred as her eyes filled with involuntary tears.

She became aware of movement and turning, she saw that Nick had come back to the open doorway, and was looking at her with interest.

'Marco wants to show you the rest of the flat,' he said.

She nodded, lifted an arm to wipe at her eyes. 'I'll be right there,' she said.

'You're crying,' he added, his voice toneless. 'Don't you like the place?'

'Like it?' She could hardly catch her breath. 'It's incredible.'

He scowled. 'A bit pokey for my taste,' he said. 'But if it meets with your approval, then...'

'It does,' she assured him. 'It's what I've always dreamed of.'

'Good. That's as it should be. Well, come along and see the rest of it before you make your mind up.' He turned away and moved out of her sight. She hesitated for just a few moments, wanting to take one last look at that incredible view, wanting to drink it in like nectar. She let out a long sigh of content. Then she turned and went back inside.

9

MOVING IN

Allie trailed dreamily after Marco as he showed her the rest of the apartment. It was all fantastic, she thought. The-state-of-the art kitchen, with its black granite worktops and stainless steel fittings; the white marble-tiled bathroom; the bedroom, with its luxurious leather ottoman bed, which could be lifted up to reveal storage for all kinds of things underneath it. There was even a small spare room with a bed, so Allie could accommodate any 'unexpected guests'.

Finally, the tour was complete and Marco asked her what she thought.

'It's perfect,' she told him. 'I love it.'

There was a short silence.

'Excellent,' he said. 'Well, we'll do the paperwork, shall we?'

Marco walked over to one of the sofas and sat down, placing his briefcase carefully on a smoked glass coffee table in front of him. He unlatched the bag, reached inside and started to pull out a sheaf of papers.

Nick settled onto the sofa beside him. 'I tell you what, Marco,' he said. 'I've got a much better idea. Let's not bother with all that fuss.'

Marco turned to look at him, puzzled. 'I'm sorry?' he said.

Nick smiled. 'Why don't we just say that we have a deal, you and I, and leave it at that?' he suggested.

'Oh, well, I'm not sure I quite underst…'

'A deal,' repeated Nick. 'A special arrangement between the two of us. What do you say?'

'I, er, suppose it's all right,' murmured Marco.

'Of course it is. And you can deal directly with me from now on, yes?'

Marco nodded, his expression one of utter confusion. 'Umm… OK…'

'And, if anybody else should express interest in this property…'

'Yes?'

'You can just tell them that it's already spoken for.' Nick placed a hand on Marco's broad shoulder and gazed deep into his eyes. 'What do you think, Marco? Would that be possible?'

Marco seemed to consider carefully for a moment. Then he appeared to reach a decision and he said, 'Yes, of course. Absolutely no problem.'

Nick's smile deepened into a grin. 'Good. So, why not give Allie her keys and you can be on your way?'

Marco nodded. He seemed somehow reassured. He reached into his pocket and took out two sets of keys on shiny silver fobs. He handed them to Allie. 'I hope you're very comfortable here,' he said earnestly. He took a business card from his top pocket. 'If anything isn't right, no matter how small, please give me a call. You'll find a welcome pack with the necessary information in the little desk drawer. Alarm codes, Wi-Fi password, all that… schizzle.' He snapped shut his briefcase and stood up. Nick did likewise.

'I'll show you to the door,' he said. 'I hope you won't mind getting a taxi back to your office, Marco, but I need Tam to take me somewhere else.'

'Absolutely no problem,' said Marco. 'A pleasure.' He and Nick shook hands. 'I'm sure your daughter will be very comfortable here,' added Marco and he and Nick walked across the room to the door. Allie stared after them in astonishment. Marco let himself out and strolled into the hallway, smiling confidently, as though he had just made the deal of the century. Nick closed the door gently behind him and turned back to see that Allie was glaring at him.

'Everything all right?' he asked her.

'Your daughter?' she whispered.

Nick chuckled. 'Yes, now you mention it, that was a rather odd thing to say,' he agreed.

'How could he think I'm your daughter when you're obviously only a few years older than me?' she cried.

'I must admit, I'm baffled,' said Nick. 'Perhaps he needs to see an optician.' The idea seemed to amuse him and he chuckled softly. 'Anyway, don't worry about that. Make yourself at home. I have other things to attend to.'

'But, wait! This doesn't make any sense.'

Nick sighed. He studied her as he might a petulant child. 'What seems to be the problem?' he asked.

'This! All this.' She gestured at her surroundings. 'People don't just walk into properties like this, not unless they're millionaires or something.'

'Apparently they do,' he corrected her.

'My parents have worked most of their lives and they haven't got anything as swish as this. And what was that stuff about the paperwork? He needed us to sign things but we didn't do it. And now, I can just live here?'

'It certainly seems that way,' said Nick. 'Look, I appreciate it's all a bit rushed, but why not give it a try? If you find that you don't really like it, we could always find something… roomier.'

74

'I don't want anything roomier! This place is like a dream home. I love it! But what if somebody comes and throws me out of here? What if they say it's all been some terrible mistake? What if the police turn up?'

'They won't,' he told her. 'You heard Marco, he and I have a deal. So kindly stop worrying and let me take care of the wee details. Now look, I really must get on. I need to go and visit your parents in Killiecrankie, who I'm sure live in a perfectly nice house.'

'My parents?' Allie glared at him. 'You're kidding, right?'

'No, not at all. Think about it, Allie, they'll be worried about you. They'll doubtless have contacted the police, there'll be all kinds of awkward questions being asked. So I need to go and explain what's happening. Calm the troubled waters, so to speak.'

'You really think they'll listen to you?'

'Of course. People generally listen when I talk.' He seemed to remember something. 'Oh, by the way, somebody will be calling here soon.'

'They will?'

'Yes. I thought it best that you have some kind of companion, you know, just to make sure you don't get into trouble. She'll be a wee bit older than you, but not so old that you can't be friends with her. I'm sure the two of you will get along famously.'

Allie wasn't sure she wanted to share her dream apartment with anyone, but then told herself she didn't exactly want to be completely alone either.

'So, er, what's she called?'

He looked vaguely perturbed by the question. 'Not sure what she's calling herself these days, but don't worry, she'll do the introductions. It'll be the start of a wonderful friendship, I have no doubt of that.'

'I'm really not sure about this. What if I don't get on with her?'

'Of course you'll get on with her! I haven't just chosen somebody at random, you know. And besides, if you don't care for her, I can easily get somebody else.'

'What, you'd just tell her she doesn't measure up?

'Something like that.'

'Okay. Look, before you go…'

'Yes?'

'I don't suppose you could let me have some money?'

He looked baffled by the question. 'Why on earth would you want money?' he asked her, as though she'd asked him for a giraffe.

'Well, it's just…'

'Go on?'

'I haven't eaten anything since breakfast, and I'm kind of hungry.'

He made a dismissive snorting sound. 'For goodness sake, girl, there's a refrigerator in the kitchen.'

'Yes, I saw it before. But obviously, it's empty.'

'Nonsense!'

'No, really, I looked in it when Marco was showing me around. There's absolutely nothing in there.'

'I'd check again if I were you,' he said confidently. 'Anyway, time waits for no man. I'll catch up with you later.' He turned and walked across the lounge to the door. 'Be good. And listen for your visitor!' He let himself out into the hallway and pulled the door shut behind him.

Allie stood for a moment, staring at the door, half-expecting it to open and for him to put his head back in and announce a change of plan. But she heard the clicking of his cane on the marble tiles outside as he walked to the lift and then there was silence. Allie sighed, shook her head and strolled into the kitchen, telling herself that this time, Nick had to be wrong. She had opened the fridge door only a few minutes earlier and there had been nothing in there, not a single thing, not so much as an ice cube tray. She took hold of the stainless steel handle and pulled the door open again.

And, somehow, she wasn't really surprised to see that the interior of the fridge was now packed with food – she saw milk and eggs and pizza and chicken legs and a salad crisper that was absolutely rammed with vegetables and fresh fruit. She stood looking at it all for a moment in mute amazement; and then, on impulse, she moved over to the nearest food cupboard and opened that too. Inside stood ranks of tinned and packet food, the labels uniformly arranged to display their contents to the world. She shook her head.

'No way,' she muttered. 'This was empty too. I know it was.'

She closed the cupboard door and went back to the fridge. After some deliberation, she took out a pepperoni pizza. She removed it from its packaging, glanced at the instructions and worked out how to switch on the oven. She slid the pizza onto a shelf, closed the door and then stood back, wondering what she might do for the fifteen minutes it would take for her lunch to be ready.

Then the doorbell rang and she walked doubtfully back into the lounge, unsure whether or not she should answer. She reminded herself that Nick had said somebody would call, but this quickly? What if it was Marco, freshly returned to his senses and wanting to know when she intended paying him some money? Worse still, what if it was the police? She pictured a uniformed man talking to her in an officious voice.

'It has come to our attention that you are living here under false pretences.' Her stomach performed a nervous back flip at the thought of it.

The doorbell shrilled again, a longer blast this time. Whoever was out there was very insistent. Allie wondered how whoever it was had managed to bypass the intercom down at the front of the building. She dithered for a few moments more, long enough for whoever was on the other side of the door to give the bell a third push. The sound seemed to echo around the entire building. Realising that there was nothing for it but to answer, Allie went to the door and opened it cautiously.

A tall, skinny young woman stood waiting. She had shoulder-length hair, dyed a shocking shade of red, and dark, piercing eyes. There were large silver hoops through her ears and she was dressed in a ragged black T-shirt, denim shorts and torn fishnet tights. Her feet were encased in paint-splashed Dr Martens and over one shoulder she carried a huge black leather bag. She looked at Allie for a moment and then her smile deepened into a dazzling grin, displaying a pronounced gap between her front teeth.

'You must be Allie,' she said, in what sounded like an Australian accent. 'I'm Sorcha.'

Allie stood there staring at the woman, for the moment at least, stuck for something to say. Finally, she managed to find a few words. 'Hi. Er… Nick said somebody would be calling.'

Sorcha frowned, clearly puzzled. 'Nick? Is he not calling himself Donald any more?' Yes, Allie decided, the woman was definitely Australian.

Allie shook her head. 'He said something about it being spoiled?'

'Ah yeah, that would make sense. He wouldn't like that.

Somebody else out there stealing his thunder.' There was a short uncomfortable silence and then Sorcha sniffed the air ostentatiously. 'I could be way off the mark here,' she said. 'But is there something cooking?'

Allie nodded. 'Pepperoni pizza,' she said.

'Excellent. Well, don't stand on ceremony, sweetie. Let's get inside and we can talk while you eat!'

10

SORCHA

Sorcha spent the remaining ten minutes it took for the pizza to be ready looking eagerly around the flat. She seemed to like what she was seeing.

'Oh wow!' she kept screeching. 'This place is fantastic.'

'Yeah. I literally moved in like, ten minutes ago.'

'Donald, I mean, Nick, is looking after you, I'd say. Aren't you the lucky girl? He doesn't always take this much trouble, you know.' Sorcha was walking around the lounge now, inspecting the framed abstract prints on the walls. 'These are a bit generic,' she observed, 'but you can always change them to things that are more you, if you feel like it.'

'Oh, am I allowed to do that?' Allie felt somewhat uncomfortable. She'd thought the paintings were really cool. 'Only, this is a rental, so…'

Sorcha made a dismissive sound, blowing out air between her lips. 'You can do whatever you want, honey, that's the whole point! You can paint the walls tartan if you feel like it.' She broke into a song. 'Be who you wanna be, do what you wanna do!' She giggled. 'I love that, don't you?'

'Er, I don't think I know it.'

'Doesn't matter. I heard it somewhere. On the radio, I expect.'

'Right. So, how do you know Nick?' asked Allie.

Sorcha gave her an evasive look. 'Think that pizza's ready now?' she asked. 'It certainly smells like it is.'

Allie glanced at her watch. 'Oh, yes, I expect so. Well, we'll eat, shall we?'

'No, you eat and I'll have a drink. Don't suppose you've got a bottle of wine tucked away somewhere?'

Allie led Sorcha through to the kitchen and after a bit of searching around, she managed to locate some plates and a silicone oven glove. She transferred the pizza to a serving plate and carried it over to the breakfast bar. A bit of rummaging in the drawers turned up a serviceable pizza wheel, so she sliced the sizzling cheesy disk into triangles. Meanwhile, Sorcha had a quick rummage in the fridge and managed to find a bottle of sauvignon blanc, which she opened and poured herself a large glassful. 'Can I get you one?' she asked.

Allie considered for a moment, but then remembered the first time she'd tried a sip of wine and had ended up spluttering it out in front of some friends. She shook her head. 'Is there a can of Coke in there?' she asked.

'Yeah,' said Sorcha regretfully. 'Totally up to you, of course. I'm not trying to convert you or anything.' She came over to the breakfast bar with the drinks and took a seat. 'I'm ready for this,' she said, raising the glass to her lips. 'I can't remember when I last drank something decent.' She took a large gulp, then sighed appreciatively. Allie noticed that her long fingernails were painted black with a tiny white skull and crossbones on each one. She saw Allie looking and smiled ruefully. 'I know,' she said. 'Bit of a hobby of mine. May have gone too far this time.'

'No, they're cool,' said Allie. 'Really.' She took a cautious bite of her first sizzling slice of pizza and chewed carefully. 'Sure you won't have some food? There's plenty here.'

'No, I'm watching my figure.'

Allie laughed at that. Sorcha was as skinny as a whippet. 'I'll never eat all this by myself,' she said.

Sorcha smiled and lowered her voice to a theatrical whisper. 'I won't tell anyone you wasted some,' she promised.

'But it's wrong to waste food, isn't it?'

'Aw, don't sweat it, hon. It ain't no sin to use the bin.' She thought for a moment. 'Perhaps you'd rather package up what you can't eat and distribute it to the homeless? I passed quite a few of them on the way over here.'

'No, that's OK. So, we were talking about Nick?'

'Were we?' Sorcha looked vaguely disappointed as though there were a million things she'd rather talk about, but seemed to resign herself to the idea. She took another gulp of wine. 'Well, him and me go way back,' she said.

'Can't be that far back,' reasoned Allie. 'I mean, he isn't much older than me, is he?' She thought for a moment. 'Though the guy from the estate agents, did seem to think that I was his daughter…'

Sorcha giggled at that. 'Yeah, that happens,' she said. 'You'll get used to it. He's actually a lot older than he looks. And of course, he does look different to other people.' She winked. 'Know what I mean?'

'No, not really. How does that work?'

Sorcha just shrugged her narrow shoulders. 'The guy's complicated,' she said, as though that explained everything. 'I mean, like really complicated.'

Allie frowned. 'How exactly did you meet him?'

Sorcha frowned. 'It's a pretty gloomy story,' she said.

'Well, tell me anyway.'

'OK, if you insist. See, I was in a very bad place,' she said.

'What? Like Dundee or something?'

Sorcha let out a shriek of laughter at this. 'No, you gala! I mean, a bad place in my head. And what's so bad about Dundee, anyway?'

Allie shrugged. 'Comedians always seem to have a dig at it,' she said.

'I've been to Dundee. It ain't so bad.' Sorcha thought for a moment. 'Actually, come to think of it, I was in my home town of Newcastle, Australia, so it was a bad place in every sense of the word. Anyhow, I had gotten myself into a bit of a mess, to tell you the truth. I'd split up with a boyfriend and somehow I'd convinced myself that he was the great love of my life.' She rolled her eyes. 'With hindsight, of course, I can see that he was a complete dickhead, but he was my first big crush, so– Anyway, as men are likely to do in these situations, he let me down, big time.' She sighed, gulped down the rest of the glass of wine and topped herself up from the bottle. 'So, I let it go round and round in my head, you know, for what must have been weeks. Depression is what it was, but I didn't really know that at the time. And I started thinking bad thoughts. I started thinking about maybe doing away with myself. It got so bad that I walked out to this bridge across the local river one day and I was actually thinking about jumping off it...'

'Oh, Sorcha, no!'

'Yeah, I'm afraid so, sweetie. But, that's when Donald, I mean, Nick, came along and... he made me see things in a totally different light. He said he thought he could use me.'

'Use you?'

'Yeah, you know, to work with his clients. People like yourself.'

'People who signed a contract?'

'That's right. This wine is yummy, by the way. Good choice.'

'Is it? I don't know anything about wine and I didn't choose what's in there. You know that the fridge was empty a few moments ago?'

Sorcha chuckled. 'Yeah, that is weird at first. But again, you'll soon get used to it. In fact, you start to expect it after a while. If you ever get a fridge that doesn't refill itself, you'll be livid.' She waved her drink. 'Sure I can't I tempt you to a glass?' she asked. 'It's lovely.'

'Oh, no, I don't really drink alcohol.'

Sorcha looked outraged. 'You're kidding, right? I'm going to have to work on that. I love a challenge. How's the pizza, by the way?'

'It's great.' Allie dropped her crust and chose another slice. She had to admit it was a particularly tasty pizza. In fact, she couldn't remember ever eating a nicer one. Which was weird because, now she thought about it, she'd never been a big fan of pizza; she'd chosen this one only because it was quick and easy to prepare.

'So, what do you do for the… clients?' she asked.

'Hmm? Oh, basically I just help 'em out. Get them settled in and so forth. It's always a bit strange at first for the people who've signed.'

Allie studied Sorcha for a moment. 'Did you sign?' she asked.

'Me? Oh no, it wasn't really appropriate for me. I mean, it never came up… the option.'

'Why not?'

'I wasn't good signing material,' said Sorcha, strangely.

'So Nick pays you to help people like me, does he?'

Sorcha seemed amused by this. 'No, he doesn't pay me

exactly. But I guess it keeps me occupied. I meet some interesting people. I get to chat to them… drink their wine. You know, that kind of thing.'

'Sorcha, have I been really stupid?'

Sorcha stopped drinking for a moment. 'Whatever do you mean, sweetie?'

'Signing that contract and everything. Is there going to be some terrible price to pay in the end?'

Sorcha swallowed a mouthful of wine. 'Nah,' she said. 'Not really. And you don't want to be worrying about all that. No, most of the people I work with have a brilliant time. Big laughs all the way.'

'Julia told me that some people come to regret signing.'

Sorcha pulled a sour face. 'Julia! You don't want to be listening to her. She'd take the shine off anything, she would. She'd make a glass of Prosecco go flat. A proper misery.'

'She seemed nice!'

'Oh yeah, I appreciate that's how she comes across, but… well, let's just say that appearances can be deceptive. Julia specialises in being a full time sour grape. If it was an Olympic event, she'd be world champion.'

'I don't really get what the deal is there. I mean, I appreciate that Nick's her son, but who's her husband? The wee girl I met, Babette. She said that her dad was called Mahoon or something? Is that a foreign name?'

'Oh, no, it's Scottish. Very traditional, actually. You should Google it.'

'I'd love to but my phone's dead. I don't suppose you have one I can use?'

Sorcha shook her head. 'Sorry babes. I haven't.' She thought for a moment. So, you met little Babette, did you? You were honoured. They usually keep her under wraps.'

'She came into my room and woke me up.'

'Did she now? Lucky you!' Sorcha waggled her eyebrows. 'Let's just say that Babette is like her mother. An acquired taste. I'm not that keen on kids myself. I'm far too selfish for all that stuff.' Sorcha made a dismissive gesture with one garishly manicured hand. 'Anyway, don't worry too much about that bunch. They like to stay up there in the old homestead. They won't be bothering us here in the big city. Not their style.'

Allie dropped another crust onto her plate, noting as she did so that Sorcha seemed to be very adept at not exactly answering her questions.

'I don't really understand,' she said. 'Who is Nick?'

Sorcha gave her a cool, studied look. 'I think you know who he is,' she said. 'I think you've always known.' She swallowed the last of the wine, wiped her mouth on the back of her wrist and clapped her hands together, signalling that the conversation was over. 'Right,' she said. 'No use sitting around here, yapping. We've got things to do!'

'What things?'

'Well, we need to get you ready, don't we?' She waved a hand at Allie's hair. 'We'll need to get that sorted for a start,' she said. 'I mean, don't get me wrong, sweetie, it's very Rebecca of Sunnybrook Farm and all that...'

'Rebecca who?'

'...but I think we need something a little bit more radical, don't you?' She reached out and stroked the sleeve of Allie's dress. 'And you'll need some decent clothes, of course. We can't have the next big star of the theatre going out dressed like that, can we? Oh, and some suitable footwear, of course. I passed a place in Bruntsfield, had some really radical shoes in the window. I reckon I can get you a discount!'

'But, I don't…' Allie had been about to say that she didn't have any money but she was beginning to understand that such considerations were meaningless now. Maybe Sorcha had funds of her own – or maybe, like Nick, she had ways of obtaining things without the need for any payment.

Sorcha stood up from the breakfast bar. 'Well, come on, tardy-pants, time waits for no-one and it won't wait for us. Cram the last of that pizza into your gob and shake a leg.'

'We're going now?'

'Why not? Is there something else you need to do?'

'Er… no, but what about Nick?'

'What about him?'

'I'm not sure where he is. He said something about going to see my parents, but, what if he needs to get in touch? He doesn't even use a mobile.'

'Oh, don't worry about that. If he needs you, he'll turn up.'

'How will he do that, exactly?'

'He'll just follow his nose.'

Allie instinctively lifted an arm to sniff at her pit. 'Are you saying I need to take a shower?'

Sorcha gave a shriek of laughter. 'No, you gala! I'm saying he has ways and means. We should shake a leg. There's lots to do. Grab your stuff and we'll split. Oh, and you might want to switch that oven off before you go.'

'Oh yeah, I forgot.' Allie turned away and twisted the dial back to the 'off' position. When she turned back, Sorcha was already striding through into the lounge so Allie grabbed a last slice of pizza and followed her. She picked up her rucksack from where she'd dropped it by the sofa. Sorcha studied it critically, noticing the embroidered name.

'Not sure about that,' she said. 'The name thing.'

'My mother did it. She's a bit of a wizard with the

sewing machine.'

'Is she now? Well, I'm sure it cuts a rug in Killiecrankie, but it won't do here. I think we'll add Moschino to the shopping list.'

'Moschino? What's that?'

Sorcha grinned delightedly. 'Such innocence,' she said. 'You have to love it. Come on, first stop, Bruntsfield.' She started towards the door and Allie remembered to grab the keys from the coffee table where Marco had left them.

'How will we get there?' she asked. 'Do we need to book a taxi or something?'

Sorcha shook her head. 'No, sweetie. You're in Edinburgh now. And when you need to go anywhere in Edinburgh, you just walk!'

The two of them stepped out into the hallway, closing the door behind them.

11

A NEW LOOK

Allie looked into the hairdresser's mirror and didn't really know what to say. As they'd walked up to Bruntsfield, Sorcha had persuaded her to try something different. 'You need something cuttin' edge, if you'll forgive the pun,' she'd explained, waving a hand at Allie's shoulder-length tresses. 'I mean, don't get me wrong, sweetie, this is very nice, but it's a bit... twentieth century, don't you think? A bit... Christian.'

'I've always worn my hair like this,' Allie had protested.

'Yeah, and that's my point. This is going to be a brand new you. Besides, it'll make it easier for wigs and stuff.'

'Wigs?'

'Sure. Actors wear wigs all the time, don't they? So you're going to need something short and radical.'

'I really don't know about that. I've never had short hair.'

'Then this is the perfect time to try it out.'

Sorcha had kept on at her and Allie had reluctantly gone along with it in the end, particularly when Juan, the hairdresser, had backed up everything Sorcha said. Juan was maybe thirty years old, Allie thought, and despite that exotic name he had a local accent. He wore his hair in a vivid purple Mohican and had the kind of ear piercings that incorporated shiny black rings the size of curtain hoops into the lobes. For good measure, there was also what looked like an ebony claw pushed through his septum.

'Well,' he said, 'what do you think?'

Allie didn't really know what to think. The face staring impassively back at her seemed somehow to have aged a couple of years and in the process gained a new sense of authority. Her honey brown hair had been clipped shockingly short on the left side of her head and swept down on the right to just above her eye. She had to admit it did look kind of distinctive but the severity of it almost made her want to cry.

'Don't you think–?' She struggled to find the right words. 'Don't you think it looks a wee bit lop-sided?'

Juan grinned, displaying dazzling white teeth. 'Yeah,' he said. 'That's exactly what it is. Asymmetric.'

'It looks killer,' said Sorcha, who was sitting on a sofa a short distance away, leafing through a glossy magazine. 'Tell her, Juan.'

'It looks killer,' echoed Juan, parrot-like.

Allie was uncomfortably aware of another young woman sitting on the sofa beside Sorcha and looking daggers at Allie, because her appointment had been unceremoniously shunted back an hour to accommodate the two newcomers who had simply turned up out of the blue, demanding to see Juan. He clearly had a thing about Sorcha. Allie had the distinct impression that had she suggested he might like to lick his fingers and stick them into an electrical socket, he'd have gone along with it without hesitation. When Allie got up to leave she was presented with a goodie bag full of shampoos and conditioners to ensure that her new hairstyle stayed looking every bit as perfect as it was now and, of course, there was never any mention of payment. Juan's only reward was a brief hug from Sorcha and a chaste peck on the cheek. 'Don't leave it so long, next time,' he told her. 'It must be what… three years since I last saw you?'

'You know how it is, sweetheart,' said Sorcha. 'Busy, busy, busy.' And with that, she led Allie out into the street.

They walked a few hundred yards along the road to a shoe shop, where Sorcha found another admirer, this one female, a punky-looking girl called Kate, with cropped black hair. She was dressed in a black T-shirt and torn denims and though Allie suspected that this one hadn't actually met Sorcha before, still she acted as though she'd just found her soulmate, saying how much she loved Sorcha's look, before patiently helping Allie to try on a whole selection of footwear, from chunky Doc Martens to patent leather evening shoes, the heels so ridiculously high that Allie could barely take three safe steps in them. Finally, Sorcha calmly informed Kate that they'd take four different pairs and Kate had dutifully packed them into boxes, which she placed into expensive-looking carrier bags. Again, there was no mention of any money. Kate gave Sorcha a fierce hug, begged her to come back soon, and Allie and Sorcha headed back out into the street carrying their spoils

'This is unreal,' said Allie.

Sorcha gave her a quizzical look. 'Don't you like shopping?' she asked.

'I don't mind it,' admitted Allie. 'But, usually I have to pay for what I buy.'

Sorcha chuckled. 'Ah, you'll soon get used to it,' she assured Allie. 'I have to say, it's much easier this way. None of that fiddling with purses and trying to remember credit card numbers. Who needs that anyway?'

Allie glanced at Sorcha's battered, paint-splashed Docs. 'How come you didn't get anything for yourself?' she asked.

'Oh…' Sorcha shrugged. 'I'm a girl of simple needs,'

she said. 'And besides, today is all about you. Now,' She glanced at her watch. 'I think we'll head into the New Town. You need clothes.'

'Do I?'

'Well sure, we're going for a complete look, aren't we? You can't have incredible hair and amazing shoes and then be seen in that.' She waved a hand disparagingly at Allie's jeans, T-shirt and jacket. 'No offence, sweetie, but if we're going to do this thing, we can't settle for half measures.'

'But I like to be casual,' insisted Allie. 'You're casual.'

'Yeah, but there's casual and there's cool casual. That's what you wear when you want to take this city by storm. No, we'll head up to Harvey Nicks. They have personal dressers there, one of them will sort you out.' She glanced at her watch. 'And we can pick up some dinner in the brasserie, afterwards.' She looked around at the busy street. 'We need a taxi,' she said.

'I thought you said in Edinburgh you walk everywhere?'

'Yeah, but not when you're carrying all these bloody boxes.' Sorcha caught a glimpse of a black cab moving along the street and raised a hand to wave at it. 'Hey!' she yelled. 'Taxi!'

The result was dramatic. The cab slammed on its brakes and car horns blared as vehicles behind were forced to take emergency evasive action. Sorcha led the way to the cab, flung open the back door and climbed in. Allie followed, trying not to notice all the angry glares she was getting from the motorists in their wake. 'Harvey Nicks,' announced Sorcha and the cab moved smoothly away, the driver's gaze fixed on the way ahead.

'Shopping is so tiring,' announced Sorcha, stifling a yawn. 'But I suppose it's a necessary evil.'

'I've never really done much of it,' admitted Allie. 'Never had the money.'

Sorcha rolled her eyes. 'Money can be an inconvenience,' she admitted. 'But when you work for Nick, it becomes less of a problem.'

'Yeah, I was going to ask about that.'

'Oh yeah? Ask away!'

'Well, how does it work, exactly? I mean, is it like you...' She lowered her voice to a whisper. '... you hypnotise people or something?'

Sorcha sniggered. 'Whatever do you mean?' she asked.

'Well, like the hairdresser, and the girl in the shoe shop? Neither of them asked for any payment.'

'Uh huh. Well, I know Juan, of course. I worked around Edinburgh for a while a few years ago. The other one – well, I guess she just liked me. People do tend to like me. I'm not sure why, it's not as if I'm friendly or anything. In fact, if I'm in one of my moods, I can be a regular crab, you know what I mean?'

'Well, that's kind of weird, isn't it? How do you stop them from asking for money?'

'I don't stop them exactly. I just never mention it.'

'But, they're working in shops. Shops are supposed to ask for money, aren't they? That's how it usually works.' She glanced briefly at the driver on the other side of the glass partition. She lowered her voice. 'When we get to wherever we're going, he's going to want paying, isn't he?'

Sorcha frowned. 'Oh sure. The idea will be there in his head. It's sort of hotwired into people. The trick is to bypass that wiring by imagining him not asking for money.'

Allie looked at Sorcha doubtfully. 'And that works?'

'Seems to. Here, tell you what…' The cab was already pulling to a halt outside a big department store. Sorcha shot Allie a sly look. 'Why don't you handle this bit?' she suggested.

'What do you mean, "handle it"?' asked Allie, alarmed.

'I mean, why don't you take care of not paying for the ride. It's really easy. Just do what I said.'

'I don't think I…'

But Sorcha had already thrown open her door and grabbed some of the bags. As Allie stared helplessly after her, she strode towards the glass doors of Harvey Nichols. Allie collected the rest of the bags and climbed sheepishly out, horribly aware that the cab driver's window was open and that he was looking expectantly at her.

'That'll be four quid,' he said.

Allie turned and stooped to look guiltily in at him. 'I'm sorry?' she murmured.

He was still looking at her. 'Four pounds,' he said again, and this time, he lifted a hand, his palm turned upwards. Allie fought a rising tide of panic. She tried to imagine what Sorcha had told her to imagine, tried to picture the hard-faced cabbie deciding that he didn't really want payment.

'Er… I… umm… have a nice day,' she ventured and he looked vaguely puzzled for a moment, as though she'd spoken in a foreign accent. Then he seemed to come to a decision. He smiled, nodded, as though perfectly satisfied with her response.

'You too,' he said. The window slid upwards again and the taxi moved away from the kerb. Allie stood there staring after it, trying to work out exactly what had just happened. She turned her head towards the store and there was Sorcha, standing in the open doorway, grinning back at her.

'See,' she said. 'Told ya. Easy as anything.' She beckoned with her free hand. 'Come on, let's get to it.'

'Weird,' murmured Allie and she followed Sorcha into the store.

12

DINNER FOR TWO

Two hours later, they slumped into seats at one of the tables in the Forth Floor Brasserie that looked down through plate glass windows onto St. Andrew Square. Allie couldn't help noticing that Sorcha had selected a table for four, even though there were just the two of them. They had bought so many clothes that Allie wouldn't actually be able to carry them all and Sorcha had somehow persuaded Ruby, their personal shopper, to take them all off their hands, promising to have them delivered later on. Allie was pretty sure that this wasn't a service generally offered by the store but she wasn't going to quibble about it. She perused the menu, realising as she did so that despite eating half a pizza for lunch, she was pretty hungry.

'Order whatever you like,' suggested Sorcha.

'Aren't you going to have anything?' Allie asked her.

'Nah, I'm not hungry. But I'll definitely take some white wine.' She gave Allie a sly look. 'Fancy splitting a bottle with me?'

'I shouldn't really,' murmured Allie. 'I'm only sixteen.'

Sorcha fixed her with a look. 'I won't tell anyone if you don't,' she said, in an exaggerated whisper, and then she laughed.

'I suppose you must think I'm really naïve,' said Allie, embarrassed.

Sorcha smiled, shook her head. 'Nah, that's OK. It's kind of refreshing, if you want to know the truth. Most of the people I meet are a long way from naïve. I guess your parents didn't let you out much, eh?'

'Not really. I suppose they wanted to protect me.' Allie glanced quickly around. 'All right,' she said, feeling suddenly bolder. 'Why not? I'll have some white wine with you.'

'Good girl.' Sorcha raised a hand and a young male waiter, en route to another table with a tray of drinks, did an abrupt about-turn and came straight over to them. He was dark-haired and rather handsome and he bowed slightly as he spoke. 'What can I get for you ladies?' he enquired.

'A bottle of white,' said Sorcha. 'Preferably something Australian.'

'There's a rather nice New Zealand Sauvignon,' said the waiter.

'Yeah, that's close enough, I reckon. And bring my friend here a selection of food, will ya?'

The man looked at Allie, puzzled. 'Care to narrow it down a bit?' he asked.

'Er… well, I…'

'You just bring her what you think she'll enjoy,' suggested Sorcha. 'You look like a man of excellent taste. Use your initiative.'

'Very good, Madam.' The waiter turned politely away and headed back to the bar area, ignoring the outraged looks of the middle-aged couple at the table he'd originally been headed for, who were still waiting for their drinks.

'I wish I was confident like you,' said Allie. 'You just told him what to do and he did it.'

Sorcha grinned. 'It comes with practice,' she said. 'I

generally find that most people want to please you. You just have to give 'em room to do it.' She picked up her handbag and rummaged around in it for a moment, then pulled out a packet of cigarettes and a lighter.

'Oh,' said Allie. 'Sorcha, I'm pretty sure you can't do that in here!'

'Think so?' Sorcha shrugged, then waved a hand at another waiter, a woman this time. 'Here, darlin', fetch us an ashtray, will ya?'

The woman turned obediently on her heels and hurried off towards the bar. By the time Sorcha had removed a cigarette from the pack and lit up, the woman was back with a small china bowl which she put down on the table without comment before moving away again. Allie glanced nervously around, registering the outraged expressions of customers at other tables, but Sorcha seemed undeterred. 'You want one of these bad boys?' she asked innocently.

Allie shook her head. 'I don't smoke,' she said. 'And you shouldn't either, Sorcha. They're really bad for you. Every time you have one of those things you take ten minutes off your life.'

Sorcha giggled. 'Is that a fact?' she murmured. 'I never knew that.' But she carried on smoking the cigarette, so Allie tried to put it out of her mind. Then the young waiter came back with the wine and a metal bucket on legs, which clinked and clattered with the sound of ice cubes. He showed Sorcha the label. 'Would madam care to try it?' he asked.

'Ah, don't stand on ceremony,' Sorcha advised him. 'Just fill the glasses and go and see about some food for my friend here, will ya?'

The young man nodded, filled the glasses and set the

rest of the bottle down in the ice bucket. He moved quickly back towards the bar, ignoring the frantic waves from the couple at the other table who still didn't have their order.

Sorcha raised her glass. 'Well, here's to gainful employment,' she said. 'Cheers!'

'Cheers.' Allie raised her own glass and took a cautious sip. Some of her friends had sworn to her that this stuff was delicious but to her it was like swigging a mouthful of vinegar. She tried not to grimace and told herself she'd probably get used to it in time. 'Am I going to hell?' she asked Sorcha, anxiously.

Sorcha looked puzzled. 'Aren't you being a little over-dramatic?' she asked. 'It's only a glass of wine.'

'That's not what I meant. I'm talking about the contract.'

'Sweetie, we're all going to hell,' said Sorcha, with a sly wink. 'It's just that some of us will get there a little bit sooner than others.' She waved her glass. 'Now, just relax and enjoy the ride.'

Allie frowned. She forced herself to take another sip of the wine. It still tasted awful. 'Tell me a bit about yourself,' she suggested.

'Not much to tell,' said Sorcha. 'Like I said before, I had this fairly miserable childhood in Australia…'

'Oh, but it's supposed to be lovely there, isn't it? Blue skies, beaches, surfing?'

Sorcha smirked. 'Not in Newcastle, New South Wales,' she said. 'Place was a freakin' dump. A coal mining area, if you want to know the truth, but of course, when people stopped using coal, everything went right down the dumper. Really high unemployment. What they call a centre of social deprivation. The only thing that ever came out of there were a couple of decent stand up comedians and that's only because they used the misery of the area as research for their jokes.' She thought for a moment. 'What else is there to say? My dad was a drunk, my mother was an idiot who spent her life trying to please him. I had one older brother who seemed to want to follow in my dad's footsteps, all the way to his favourite bar...' She shook her head. 'It's not a pretty picture. What about you, sweetcakes?'

'Oh, well, I was going to say my childhood was miserable until I heard about yours,' she admitted. 'Mine was just... dull, I suppose.'

The young waiter reappeared brandishing a plate, which he set down in front of Allie. 'For your starter, madam, I chose the soy-marinated salmon with wasabi mayonnaise and puffed rice. I hope it meets with your approval.'

'It looks great,' said Allie, though she really wasn't sure if she'd ever eaten anything like it before. The waiter smiled and moved away again. This time, he did register the frantic gesticulations from the other table and moved reluctantly across to it. The man at the table started talking rapidly in the waiter's ear, occasionally pausing to point at Sorcha in apparent disgust. The waiter listened for a moment and then said something in return, before heading off towards the bar. The man sat there, open-mouthed, looking horrified. Then he stood up, took his jacket from the back of the chair and put it on. He said something to the woman sitting next to him and she too put on her coat. As they moved briskly towards the exit, Allie caught a snatch of something the man was saying. 'Absolutely outrageous! I can't believe he spoke to me like that–'

But then they were gone. Sorcha meanwhile, seemed completely oblivious to the exchange. She was concentrating on gulping down large mouthfuls of wine and puffing contentedly on her cigarette. Allie focused on her plate of food, lifting a forkful of salmon to her mouth. She had to admit, it tasted reassuringly expensive, but the dollop of green stuff on the side of the plate was much too hot for her liking.

'Just leave it if you don't like it,' Sorcha advised her. 'I expect he'll be bringing you something else in a minute.'

'No, it's quite nice, actually. Just… unusual.' Allie lifted her glass and took another sip of the wine. This time, she thought, she had more of a sense of the flavour of it, something fruity underneath that initial vinegar kick.

'So,' she mused. 'How long ago did you start working for Nick? You said you'd just split up with your boyfriend when you first met him. So you were, what, late teens, early twenties?'

Sorcha nodded. 'Sure,' she agreed. 'Something like that.'

'But you also said that the two of you go back a long way.'

'Yeah, I did say that.'

'But here's the thing, Sorcha. You can't be much more than that now.'

There was a silence then. Sorcha seemed to be considering the best way to answer. She looked at the smouldering end of her cigarette for a moment, then took a deep breath. 'You know how I said that Nick is older than he looks?'

Allie nodded.

'Well, so am I, sweetie. A lot older. Personally, I put it down to leading a blameless life.'

The waiter appeared again, with another plate. 'I thought madam might care for a little salad,' he announced. 'This is the chargrilled chicken Caesar with parmesan croutons and anchovy dressing. Enjoy.' He set the plate down beside the one that Allie was still eating from, bowed his head and walked away again.

'I haven't even finished the salmon yet,' whispered Allie.

Sorcha spread her hands in a 'what can you do?' expression. 'He's evidently keen to impress,' she said. She winked. 'Hey, play your cards right and you could be in there!'

Allie giggled, then made an attempt to recover her train of thought. 'So, when you say, "older", how much are we talking about? Five years? Ten years?'

Sorcha was about to reply when she looked up and her eyes widened in sudden recognition. Allie turned to see Nick coming towards their table, his long black satin coat skimming the carpeted floor around him. Behind him, looking uncomfortably out of place, walked a young man dressed in a casual floral shirt, blue jeans and open-toed sandals. He wore spectacles and had longish, untidy hair. A shabby canvas bag hung over his shoulder.

'Ah, here you are!' said Nick, treating them like a couple of long-lost friends. 'I had a feeling I'd find you here. I hope you don't mind if we join you.' He gestured to his young companion who came around the table and slipped into the vacant chair beside Allie. He nodded sheepishly to the two women at the table, looking as though he'd rather be anywhere else instead. Nick sank into the other spare seat beside Sorcha. 'I trust you two have been getting along famously together,' he said.

'We're getting on like gangbusters,' said Sorcha and Allie couldn't help noticing that all of her assurance seemed to have vanished. She looked wary, defensive, as though sensing imminent criticism.

Nick studied Allie critically for a moment and then waved a hand at Sorcha 'This is the kind of hair that will get her noticed?' he murmured.

'Absolutely,' said Sorcha.

'Well, I'll have to take your word for that. To me it looks… lop-sided.'

'That's what I said!' muttered Allie.

'It's asymmetric,' Sorcha assured him. 'It's all the rage, right now.'

Nick's gaze fell on the glass of wine beside Allie's plate. He frowned and directed a fierce glare at Sorcha. 'When I told you to entertain the girl, I assumed you understood what I meant by that,' he said. 'I don't want you to encourage her in bad habits. That's not why I summoned you. And put out that vile-smelling cigarette immediately!'

Sorcha bowed her head and did exactly as she was told. She looked somehow like a dog that had just been shouted at. Nick reached out a hand, lifted Allie's glass of wine and leaned across the table to place it in front of the young man. 'Justin, I'm sure you'll enjoy a drink with your meal,' he purred. He looked quickly around the room. His gaze fell on the young waiter and he nodded his head in the man's direction. Nick didn't actually say anything, but the waiter reacted as though he'd been prodded with something sharp. He hurried away, only to reappear moments later, carrying another tray. This one contained an empty wine glass and a tumbler filled with what looked like cola. Nick took the latter and set it carefully down beside Allie's plate. She stared at it resentfully, wondering what made Nick think he could dictate what she had to drink. The waiter lifted the bottle of wine and filled the empty glass. Nick took this, tasted the wine and nodded his head. 'Splendid,' he said. 'Now, I would like you to bring my young friend, Justin, a selection of your finest food. Use your own judgement.'

'Very good, sir.' The waiter bowed, a strangely formal gesture, Allie thought, and hurried away. There was a silence around the table then, while everybody waited for somebody to say something. Eventually it was Nick who spoke first.

'Now, before I forget, Allie, your parents send you their love.'

'They do?' Allie stared at Nick in disbelief. 'Really?'

'Absolutely. They are thrilled by this new departure and wish you every success with it.'

Allie shook her head. 'What did you tell them?' she asked.

'That you have your mind set on a new career. I told them that I have become your manager and I will ensure you have nothing but the very best care and attention. I gave them my solemn promise in that regard.'

'And they were happy with that?'

'Of course they were. Why wouldn't they be? People are generally happy with what I tell them. They've also agreed to call off the dogs.'

'The dogs?'

'The police. As I suspected, your parents had reported your sudden departure to them. But I was able to reassure them that it was merely a misunderstanding. So that's all taken care of.' Nick waved a hand in a gesture of dismissal. 'Now, I hope you don't mind, Allie, but I have invited a rather special guest to dine with us,' he said. 'Allow me to introduce my new friend, Justin.'

Justin smiled awkwardly at Allie and raised his glass to her. 'Hi,' he said.

'I'm pleased to meet you,' said Allie, bewildered.

'I'm sure you will be even more pleased when I tell you who Justin is,' said Nick, smiling. He left the statement hanging for a moment as though expecting Allie to reply, but she didn't really know what to say, so she just smiled vacantly and shrugged her shoulders.

Nick took a deep breath. 'Justin is a prize-winning young playwright,' he said. 'Justin is about to have his debut play performed at a local theatre. And I've been telling Justin all about you.' Nick leaned a little closer and his smile deepened. 'You see, Allie, at the present time, he is missing just one vital ingredient for his show. He's looking for a leading lady.'

13

DINNER FOR FOUR

Allie let that information sink in for a moment. She wasn't at all sure how she was supposed to react to Nick's remark. In the end, only one word seemed appropriate. 'Wow,' she said.

'Wow indeed,' purred Nick. 'So, Justin, why don't you tell us a little bit more about your project?'

Justin seemed to consider for a moment, as though he wasn't entirely sure what his 'project' actually was. Or perhaps he was just reluctant to talk about it. He took a sip of his wine, as though preparing himself to speak. When he finally did, Allie noted, he had a fairly posh Edinburgh accent.

'Well,' he said, 'I entered this competition. It was run by the Scottish Book Trust…'

'Oh, a wonderful institution,' said Nick. 'We're great fans, aren't we, Allie?'

'Uh huh.' Allie was so mesmerised she had to remind herself to push a forkful of food into her mouth. She'd never heard of the Scottish Book Trust and was pretty sure that Nick hadn't either, but she wasn't about to admit the fact.

'And the way it worked,' continued Justin, 'was that you were invited to submit the first ten pages of a novel, a play or a screenplay. I chose to do a play.'

'Good move,' murmured Nick.

'Er, yeah, so I had this idea about a teenage girl who

has this, well, I suppose you'd call it a vision. It's set in medieval times, you know, and she's sort of like this very simple country girl who one day has a vision of a man stepping out of a glowing sphere. And she tells her parents about it and, of course, they tell other people and eventually word gets around her village and she becomes this kind of local phenomenon. And everybody thinks she's had a religious experience, you know, that she's seen some kind of a saint or whatever, but of course it's entirely obvious to us, the audience, that what she's actually seen is a time traveller.' He looked around the table as though eliciting some kind of reaction and Allie thought she'd better say something so she said, once again, 'Wow.' And then she added: 'That's cool.'

'Yeah, well, it's just a one act thing,' said Justin, as though trying to play it down. 'But part of the prize was to get it produced and put on at the Traverse...' He paused. 'You do know the Traverse, I suppose?'

There was a brief silence before Sorcha took the initiative.

'Are you kidding?' she cried. 'Of course we know the Traverse. We love the Traverse, don't we, guys?'

Allie and Nick nodded enthusiastically.

'Well, it is recognised as the theatre for new writing in Scotland,' said Justin. 'And obviously, this is a big opportunity for me, so–'

'The interesting thing,' interrupted Nick, looking at Allie, 'is that Justin was telling me earlier, that they are still looking for somebody to play the lead role in–' He glanced at Justin. 'What's it called again?'

'*Rapture*.'

'Yes, *Rapture*. Love the title by the way! Anyhow, it turns out there's an open audition tomorrow.'

'Ah, no.' Justin was shaking his head. 'No, there's an audition, right enough, but it's not an open one. We're looking at some possible actors to play the part of Theresa and we've had quite a bit of interest–'

'But obviously you're going to make the time to see Allie,' Nick told him.

'Well, I can't promise anything,' Justin reminded him. 'I mean, it's really not up to me, is it? There's a producer and a director. I'm only...'

'... the man who created the whole thing!' finished Nick, bombastically. 'Of course you will have a say. It would be a travesty if you didn't.'

'Erm, well, I expect we might be able to work something out...'

Just then, the young waiter arrived holding a plate of food. 'I thought Sir might like to start with the crispy Camembert with apple and radish salad,' he said, and placed the food in front of Justin. Justin stared down at it for a moment as though he'd never seen anything quite like it before. 'Looks... great,' he said. He glanced up at the others. 'I'm not used to this,' he warned them. 'I can't usually afford more than the local takeaway.'

'Oh, we'll have to do something about that,' said Nick. 'We can't have our rising literary stars eating like peasants.'

'Oh no, I'm not saying that! It's just that I'm usually a man of simple tastes. But this looks fabulous.' Justin picked up his knife and fork and started to eat enthusiastically. When he spoke again, it was with a mouth that was crammed with food. 'I'm only saying that of course I can mention Allie's name, but that doesn't mean that they'll see her for the role. Like I said, there's been a lot of interest. The schedule's pretty full.'

Nick smiled confidently. 'I don't doubt it,' he said. 'But look, why don't we come along tomorrow and just see how it goes? I feel sure that when your team sees what Allie is capable of, they'll be convinced she'd be perfect for the role. Did I tell you that she's just starred in *The Crucible*?'

Justin looked at Allie with fresh interest. 'Really? Well, that's interesting. Which production was it?'

Allie swallowed a chunk of anchovy with difficulty. 'Oh, it was – it was just for the – school…'

'Schools' festival,' interrupted Sorcha. 'Countrywide. I'm sure you heard of it. Everyone who was anyone was involved. Allie won the special jury prize.'

Justin looked impressed. 'Oh yes? Where was this?' he asked.

'In London,' said Nick smoothly before Allie could even open her mouth. 'It was a huge success. But I managed to entice her up to Edinburgh. I feel sure that she'll find more rewarding roles in her homeland.'

Justin nodded. 'I love Arthur Miller,' he said. 'And *The Crucible* is one of the most powerful allegories ever written.' He looked at Allie again, as though seeing her with fresh eyes. 'Which role did you play?' he asked.

'Abigail Williams,' said Allie, more confident now she was telling something closer to the truth.

'Well, that character would be completely in tune with what you'd need for Catherine,' he said. 'Same sort of era, really. But Ayrshire, of course, rather than New England.'

'Oh, of course,' agreed Allie.

'And, as I keep saying, it's really not up to me.'

'We understand,' said Nick. He had lifted the bottle of wine from the ice bucket and was now topping up Justin's glass. 'But let me ask you this question, Justin. Who could possibly know a character better than the man who created her? Hmm? Answer me that.'

'Well, that's true enough, I suppose.' Justin raised his glass and took a generous swallow of the wine. He looked at Nick and then at Sorcha. 'So, er, how come you two aren't eating?' he asked.

'They never do,' said Allie.

'We drink though,' Sorcha reminded her, raising her own glass.

'So, Justin,' said Nick. 'Tell us a bit more about yourself. What's your background?'

'Me? Oh, well, I went to Edinburgh Uni.'

'Wonderful establishment,' purred Nick.

'I did English Literature and came out with a first. I've always dabbled with writing fiction, you understand. I tried a novel first but never quite got around to finishing it. And I'd pretty much resigned myself to a career in teaching when I saw the advert for the competition and I thought to myself, why not give it one last go?' He smiled. 'Of course, winning the prize was a big incentive. It was the kick up the backside I needed.'

'Must have been.' Nick glanced around, caught the eye of the young waiter and nodded at the bottle in the ice bucket. The waiter hurried away like an attentive hound. 'Now all your hard work is paying off,' enthused Nick. 'That fills me with happiness. Time to celebrate, I think, with something a wee bit more... bubbly. What do you say?'

Justin looked worried. 'Oh, I'd better go easy,' he said. 'There's the interviews tomorrow and I'm really not much of a drinker.'

'Nonsense,' said Sorcha, with a sly wink. 'You're doing a great job!'

'If I carry on like this, I'll be agreeing to all kinds of nonsense.'

'That's what we're counting on,' said Nick, and everyone laughed a little too loudly.

Justin took another gulp of wine and then looked at Allie, more challengingly than he had before. The drink seemed to be giving him a little more confidence. 'OK,' he said. 'So, what makes you think you'd be the right person to play the part of Catherine?'

Allie thought for a moment. 'Well, of course, I haven't seen a script or anything, but, you said yourself that Abigail Williams is the same kind of fit. And I played her like... like a musical instrument, you know? I felt like she was in my blood – as though she was oozing right out of my pores. Miss Marchmont said–'

'Miss Marchmont?' Justin raised his eyebrows and Allie felt a twinge of panic rising up in her.

'Emily Marchmont,' said Sorcha, slipping into the invention as though it was as easy to her as breathing. 'The drama critic for *The Times*? Now what was it she said about your performance, Allie? Something like–?'

'An astonishing new star is born,' offered Nick, smiling pleasantly. 'Something to that effect wasn't it?'

Now it was Justin's turn say the word. 'Wow. *The Times*? How recently was this?'

'Just last month,' said Sorcha. 'We were very pleased, weren't we, Allie?'

'Er... yeah. Dead pleased.' Allie didn't really see how she could say anything else, but she felt a jolt of disquiet go through her. She would much rather have stuck to the truth. She hated all this invention. And yet, she told herself, what was the problem? She had been really good as Abigail, and she was predicted an A for her exam...

The young waiter turned up with a bottle of champagne and some tall glasses. He exchanged the champagne for the empty bottle in the ice bucket. Allie couldn't help wondering how he'd known not to just bring another bottle of ordinary white wine. It was as though he could read Nick's mind.

'How is everything?' he asked the diners.

'Splendid,' said Nick. He glanced at Justin. 'Now, I'd hazard a guess and say that you're a man who enjoys a steak. Would I be correct in that assumption?'

Justin looked puzzled. 'I guess so,' he said.

'Excellent.' Nick turned back to the waiter. 'I want you to bring my friend here the finest cut of steak you have on the premises,' he said. 'No half measures, mind you. I want it to be succulent. I want it to be so tender that he could slice it with a plastic knife. Do I make myself clear?'

'Yes, sir. Absolutely.' The waiter turned to Allie. 'And for madam?'

'Oh, I'm actually quite full now,' said Allie.

'Yes, and you're going to have to start watching your portions, anyway,' said Nick. 'Let's face it, if you're going to convince in the role of a medieval peasant girl, we can't have you looking too well-fed, can we?'

'Umm... no, I suppose not,' agreed Allie, but she felt a twinge of disappointment, because she was only really being polite and was half expecting somebody to talk her out of it. The waiter turned obediently away and Nick focused his attention back on Justin.

'And do you have any other advice for the star of your debut play?' he murmured. 'Any pointers?'

'Look, you mustn't say that!' protested Justin.

'That she needs advice?'

'No, that she's the star of my play. Nothing has been decided. I… I don't want her to be disappointed.'

'My dear fellow, don't worry on that score. Allie is a professional. She's able to deal with anything the world throws at her.' He lifted the champagne from its bucket and his hand closed around the foil-covered top. He gave it an expert twist and the cork came out with a loud pop. Sorcha held out glasses and Nick filled three of them. Then he gave Allie a sly look, as though considering and waved to Sorcha to get a fourth. 'On this one occasion, I'm going to allow you a glass,' he told Allie. 'Because this is a special toast and I don't want to leave you out.' He leaned closer to her. 'But don't get used to it,' he added. He filled another glass, handed it to her and then got to his feet, holding his own glass in front of him. He looked around the table and everybody else stood upright. 'To *Rapture*,' said Nick, and everybody drank.

It was Allie's first taste of champagne and she had to admit that it was a lot more exciting than ordinary wine. There was a sudden rush of bubbles in her mouth, which filled her head with a satisfying dizziness.

They all sat down again. Justin had drunk his entire glass down and Nick immediately leaned forward and topped him up. Allie couldn't help noticing that both Nick and Sorcha had barely taken a sip from their own glasses.

'It's really kind of you,' said Justin and his voice now sounded decidedly slurred, 'to buy me dinner and everything. Of course, I will, if I can, put in a good word for Allie, tomorrow. But in the end, it really will depend how she does, assuming she even gets an audition, of course.'

'Yes, I was thinking about that,' said Nick. 'Obviously, Allie hasn't even seen a script, yet. I don't suppose–' He pointed a finger at Justin's shoulder bag hanging off the back of his chair. 'You wouldn't have a copy in there, would you?'

Justin turned his head to look at the bag as though he'd forgotten he owned it. 'Well, yes,' he said. 'There is the monologue that the actors are supposed to do tomorrow, but, well, the idea is they are given it on the day and they read it cold. So that nobody has any advantage, you understand.'

Nick smiled. 'Very commendable,' he said. 'But surely, you wouldn't mind if she had a quick peek at it, would you? Tonight? So she can prepare herself for the audition.'

Justin scowled. 'I'm really not supposed to,' he murmured. He lifted his glass and took another big gulp of champagne.

'I appreciate that,' purred Nick. 'But don't you think it would be so much better if she could go over it? Wouldn't you like to hear your words performed exactly as they should be?' He was gazing directly at Justin now and Allie saw a familiar dazed look creep into the young playwright's eyes. Without saying another word, he set down his glass, unbuckled the bag and took out some sheets of printed paper. He handed them to Nick, who rolled them up and slipped them into the pocket of his coat. He waited a few moments and then coughed into his hand. Justin twitched in his chair, as though startled and his gaze became a little more focused. He didn't mention the script again and Allie had the distinct impression that he didn't even know he'd just handed it over.

'So, what time tomorrow?' asked Nick. 'At the Traverse?'

'Well, the first appointment is for ten o' clock,' said Justin. 'But I really don't think you'll be able–'

Nick waved him to silence. 'You just let us take our chances on that,' he said. 'I'm sure everything will be fine. Ah!'

The young waiter was back once more, carrying a large white plate. He set it down in front of Justin like an offering. 'My God,' said Justin. Allie could appreciate his surprise. He was looking at what must have been the biggest steak in history, a great slab of medium rare meat surrounded by onions and mushrooms and potatoes and all manner of other foodstuffs. It was more than any one person could have hoped to consume. 'The chef created this specially,' said the waiter, smiling benignly. 'That's the most expensive steak we have. A wagyu kobe. I hope it's to Sir's liking.'

Justin struggled to find words to reply. 'It... it's... fantastic,' he said.

'Indeed it is,' agreed Nick. 'Please give the chef our heartiest compliments. And you may as well bring another bottle of that excellent champagne.' He smiled confidently. 'I rather think we'll be making a night of it.'

14

AUDITION

Allie woke from a dreamless sleep and sat up in alarm, horribly aware that somebody had just climbed on to the end of her bed. Her first thought was that Babette had somehow found her way to Edinburgh, but when her bleary eyes focused she saw to her relief that it was only Sorcha, dressed in red knickers and a tattered T-shirt, carrying a tray of breakfast things.

'Come on, sleepy-head,' she drawled. 'It's your big day. You need to wake up and smell the coffee.' She slid the tray onto Allie's lap, revealing that it did indeed contain a huge mug of coffee and a bowl of cereal.

'What time is it?' muttered Allie wearily.

'Eight o' clock,' said Sorcha. 'I thought you might need a bit more time to go over that monologue before we head off to the theatre.'

'I've been over it a hundred times!' protested Allie. 'Seriously, I know it by heart.' She scowled. 'If I could only make head or tail of it, I'd be happier.'

The previous night, when they'd got back to the apartment, Sorcha had made her read through Justin's printed pages again and again, not letting her go to her room until the early hours of the morning. But Allie had struggled with it. 'It's all so... wordy,' she said.

'What do you mean?' cried Sorcha. 'Okay, so it's a bit experimental–'

'Is that what you call it? Sounds like gibberish to me!'

Sorcha shook her head. 'You heard what Justin said last night. He's written it in an authentic medieval dialect.'

'*The Crucible* didn't sound like that!'

'You've got to stop comparing everything to that one play,' Sorcha advised her. 'Justin is many things, but Arthur Miller isn't one of 'em. Anyway, it must be good. It's art. It won a prize, didn't it?'

Allie didn't have anything to say to that. She picked up a spoon and pushed some cornflakes into her mouth. She chewed for a moment then took a large gulp of coffee, feeling the caffeine begin to unravel the outer threads of her sleepiness. 'Everything's moving too quickly,' she complained.

Sorcha gave her a sympathetic look. 'I know what you mean, sweetie, but Nick isn't somebody to take his time over things. He spotted a chance and he went for it. That's how he operates.'

'Yeah, well, he might have mentioned it to me, first. I mean, who's all this supposed to be in aid of?'

'Well, you obviously, but...' Sorcha sighed. 'Listen, honey, there are kids out there who would give their right arm for the chance you've just been handed on a plate. All Nick is doing is making sure you get the right opportunities.'

'But... he was lying, last night. And so were you, for that matter! What if Justin checks up on that stuff about the schools competition, and the critic from *The Times*?'

Sorcha shook her head. 'He won't,' she said. 'People never do. They just believe what they're told. That's the beauty of it.' She chuckled. 'I wonder how Justin is this morning,' she murmured. 'He was three sheets to the wind last night. He nearly fell into that taxi we booked for him.'

Allie waved a hand. 'All that,' she said. 'I don't like it. Getting him drunk so he'll go along with things. I want to do this on my own terms.'

'Honey, you will. End of the day, all we can do is get these people to consider you. Whether you pass the audition or not, well, that's up to how good you are.'

Allie scowled. 'What if I'm not any good?' she murmured. 'What then?'

'It'll be time to go back to the drawing board, I suppose. But let's not be defeatist. I happen to believe in you. I see a big future for you, babycakes. Now…' Sorcha waved her hands impatiently. 'Shove that breakfast down yourself. We need to get you ready for the audition.'

'What does that involve?'

'Just creating the right look for you. You need to look innocent but confident. Not too needy, but not too superior. Don't worry. It won't hurt a bit. Just leave it all to your Auntie Sorcha.'

Allie swallowed another spoonful of cereal. 'Where's Nick?' she asked.

'Search me. Said he had stuff to do last night, but he'll meet us at the theatre at ten o' clock. Don't worry, it's only fifteen minutes walk from here.'

She got up off the bed and headed for the door.

'Sorcha?'

She paused, turned. 'Yes, sweetie?'

'You are coming with me, aren't you?'

'To the theatre? Sure. Wouldn't miss it. But when it's time for the audition, it'll just be you in there. That's how these things generally work.'

'Really?' Allie put down her spoon as her stomach performed a violent lurch. 'Oh God. What if I'm terrible?' she asked. 'What if I'm no good?'

'You'll be fine. Now come on, stop fretting and eat that breakfast. We need to get this show on the road.'

A couple of hours later, they strode in through the automatic swing doors of the Traverse Theatre, a clean, contemporary building off Lothian Road with lofty ceilings and a spacious foyer. Allie noticed with a twinge of alarm that about ten young women were seated on leather sofas, most of them studiously looking at their mobile phones. Allie, who hadn't been able to access her own phone since she'd first encountered Nick, couldn't help feeling a stab of envy. She'd asked Sorcha several times if she might be able to get her hands on a charger, but she had point-blank refused to help, explaining that Nick was 'very particular' about such things, that he wouldn't like it if Allie got hold of one.

Sorcha located a spare seat and led Allie over to it. They sat down, side-by-side and Sorcha studied the nearest of the girls, a skinny brunette with brightly painted orange lips. 'Hey, honey,' said Sorcha, good-naturedly. 'You here for the audition?'

The girl nodded her head and gave a guarded smile, but she didn't speak and quickly returned her attention to her mobile.

'Yeah, nice meeting you too!' said Sorcha loudly. She turned to look at Allie. 'Well, looks like we came to the right place,' she said and several of the other women lifted their heads to study Allie, as though looking at bits of dirt under their fingernails. She felt very uncomfortable under their combined gaze and was relieved when they eventually went back to looking at their phones.

'I don't like this,' she whispered and Sorcha gave her a reassuring smile.

'You'll be fine,' she said. 'Don't sweat it.' She reached into her bag and pulled out what looked like a credit card. She handed it surreptitiously to Allie. 'I nearly forgot,' she said. 'Put that in your Moschino, you might need it.'

Allie glanced at it, noting her own name and signature, a membership number and the word 'Equity' prominently printed on it.

'How did you get this?' she hissed.

'Oh, Nick pulled a few strings. He thought it'd be useful.'

Allie shook her head and slipped the card into her pocket. From what she'd heard Equity cards were harder to get hold of than an axe handle made of jelly.

The outer doors swung open and two familiar people entered. Nick, as ever, was striding confidently along, and beside him Justin was wearing dark glasses and looked rather the worse for wear. They paused in the foyer for a moment and had a brief mumbled conversation. Then Justin turned away and went down the staircase that led to the next floor, leaning heavily on the banister as he went, as though he was having trouble staying upright. Nick stood for a few seconds, looking calmly around, and then he moved closer to the group of young women. Oddly, he didn't acknowledge Allie and Sorcha, but instead kept his attention fixed on the others, appraising them. Finally, he spoke in a loud, clear voice.

'I hope everybody is feeling well enough to attend the audition, this morning,' he said calmly. 'Only, I've just heard there's been an outbreak of gastroenteritis in the area. Spreading like wildfire, I believe.' And with that, he smiled, turned away and strode back across the foyer to the doors. They swung open and he went outside.

There was a puzzled silence. The young women gave

each other baffled looks and a couple of them chuckled and shook their heads before returning their attention to their phones. Some moments passed.

'What's going on?' whispered Allie.

Sorcha shrugged. 'Haven't a clue,' she said, but her expression suggested she wasn't being entirely honest.

'Well, it must mean some…'

Allie broke off as the nearest of the women, the brunette, looked up suddenly as if she'd just heard somebody shout her name. Her eyes widened in evident surprise. She snatched in a deep breath with a gulp and got to her feet, as though she'd just woken from a particularly nasty dream. She took a couple of halting steps forward, then made a convulsive retching sound and doubled up as if in pain. She was suddenly and spectacularly sick on the floor. 'Oh my God,' she said. She stared forlornly down at the mess in front of her as though wondering where it might have come from, then staggered drunkenly towards the exit. Halfway there, she threw up again, spraying a chunky yellow tide across the pristine tiles. She let out a long groan and flailed wildly out of the doors, which after a few moments swung silently shut behind her.

Allie and Sorcha looked at each other in bewilderment. Their gaze was abruptly drawn to a second woman, a redhead, who leapt to her feet and performed similar manoeuvres to her predecessor, but she somehow managed to be sick all down the front of her white lace blouse before she made it out of there. There were groans of realisation now from the other seated women. Hands flew to mouths and stomachs were clutched as a tide of nausea overcame them. Several got up and left, picking their way carefully through the sticky puddles that already covered the floor, while those made of sterner stuff stuck it grimly out until they too were noisily projecting their breakfasts in all directions. Horrified and repulsed, Allie started to rise from her seat but Sorcha kept a firm hand on her, holding her firmly in position.

'Stick it out,' she murmured. 'You'll be fine.'

In a matter of minutes, it was pretty much all over. Aside from Allie there was just one other woman, clearly determined to stay right where she was, even though she kept making regular retching sounds. Over in the box office a couple of assistants sat behind the counter looking out in dismay, clearly wondering which of them had the responsibility of mopping up the mess that now marred their pristine workplace.

Just then, a smiling, bearded man with a clipboard under his arm appeared at the top of the stairs and stood looking into the foyer. His smile quickly faded and was replaced with a look of horror as he registered the scene of devastation before him, but he came closer, wrinkling his nose at the overpowering smell and consulted his clipboard.

'Umm… Tanya O' Donaghue?' he inquired. This was greeted with silence, so he consulted the board again. 'Er… Chloe Coltrane?' he ventured.

The one woman still remaining from the original cohort lifted an arm, her other hand clamped tightly over her mouth.

'If you'd like to come with me to the studio,' said the man, 'we're ready to…'

But Chloe was now spraying vomit in a colourful shower from between her fingers. She made a helpless groaning sound, reeled sideways and ran for the exit, puking as she went. The bearded man stared after her in open-mouthed shock. 'Er, thank you,' he said at last, and turned his attention back to the clipboard, no doubt wondering what had happened to the other people listed there. He turned his head to look at Allie and Sorcha. 'Er... are you two...?'

'Not me,' said Sorcha, quickly. She indicated Allie. 'Her. Allie Lawrence.'

The man consulted his clipboard again and seemed puzzled. Clearly her name wasn't there. Then he seemed to remember something. 'Oh wait, are you the girl that Justin mentioned? He said something about meeting you last night?'

Allie managed to find her voice. She still wasn't entirely sure that she wasn't going to be sick herself, surrounded as she was by the combined stench of other people's vomit. 'Yes, that's me,' she said weakly. 'Justin said you might be able to give me a chance to read.'

'Oh, right, well, to be honest we thought the day was pretty much spoken for, but...' He gave a last forlorn look around. 'What happened to the others?' he asked. 'I've quite a few names on my list.'

Sorcha shook her head. 'Gastroenteritis,' she said. 'Terrible. It's a regular epidemic at the moment.'

'Really? I didn't know that.' The man frowned, then looked at Allie. 'Well,' he said, 'As you're here, I suppose we may as well have a look at you. If you'd like to come with me?'

Allie nodded. She got to her feet and glanced anxiously at Sorcha.

'Go and knock 'em dead,' said Sorcha, giving her an encouraging wink.

Allie managed a smile and walked across to the bearded man, carefully negotiating the glistening pools on the tiled floor as she did so. She made it safely to the top of the staircase and she and the man began to descend side-by-side.

'So, have you driven far this morning?' he asked her, politely.

Allie shook her head and was suddenly aware of a new-found confidence brimming within her. 'This is Edinburgh,' she said. 'Wherever you need to go, you just walk.'

15

REHEARSAL

'All right, let's take it from the top, shall we?' suggested Martin.

Martin Pringle was the director of *Rapture* and it was the final week's rehearsal before the play's first performance. For Allie, the previous three weeks had sped by in a blur. She barely remembered her audition now, the way she'd recited the words she'd memorised by heart, the way the three people auditioning her had just sat there open-mouthed after she'd finished speaking, as though they'd experienced some kind of religious vision themselves. She'd known right then and there that they were going to offer her the part. She only wished that she could be sure that their reactions were genuine, that they hadn't in some way been bewitched by Nick, even though he was nowhere to be seen by then. Surely he couldn't influence people from a distance? Could he? But then she thought of the way he'd influenced her competition for the role and she knew only too well that he was quite capable of doing exactly that.

But at any rate, they had offered her the part. And of course, she'd accepted it, she'd have been crazy not to, she'd have equal billing with the other three actors starring alongside her which was a fantastic opportunity for a novice. After that she'd been plunged headlong into a frantic schedule. She'd been introduced to the other, older members of the cast, who had all behaved like they were doing her an immense favour, allowing her to act alongside them. She'd met the producer, a hippie-ish looking woman called Fran, who favoured violently-coloured dresses and large, hooped earrings; she'd met stage managers and lighting technicians and musicians and all manner of people who would be involved in the production of the play; and of course, she'd met Martin, a thin, serious-looking guy in his late forties, with cropped black hair and horn-rimmed glasses. After that, she'd embarked on a daily series of rehearsals as she and the other three cast members worked through the script of *Rapture*, trying to make it come to life, while its author, Justin, sat in the front row of the stalls, watching expressionlessly as his brainchild began to take form right in front of his eyes.

Dean was playing Theresa's father, Gregor. He was a big bluff bearded man with intense blue eyes and a booming voice that seemed to fill any room. Maggie played Theresa's mother, Flora. She was a tiny, wizened little woman with a shock of grey hair and a terribly posh English accent, which miraculously transformed into a broad Scottish one every time she spoke a line from the script. And then there was Jason, a young, lean actor who had been cast as Michael, the new priest in the area, a man who was keen to claim Theresa's vision for the glory of the church. Jason was in his twenties, extremely good-looking and very aware of the fact. Whenever his dark brown eyes looked deep into Allie's, she felt shaken to the core and had to constantly remind herself that he was only acting and that he had no interest in her whatsoever outside of the play. And yet... she did entertain the notion that one of these nights he might just ask her to go with him for a drink somewhere. But it hadn't happened yet.

'Now, before we start,' continued Martin, 'I want everybody to take a moment to put themselves into their characters... to imagine that it really is the fourteen hundreds and that this,' He gestured around at the small rehearsal room, 'really is a barn in Ayrshire.'

Martin, Allie had quickly learned, was a fan of 'the method' and liked his actors to immerse themselves in role playing, even when they were only rehearsing. At first, she had felt completely out of her depth. There were things in this play she really didn't understand, but Martin had taken great care with her, explaining everything in detail, giving her the opportunity to try different approaches, and though she still felt ill-at-ease, he seemed happy with her progress. Martin, she had been told, had directed some 'important' pieces. If she'd had access to a phone or a computer, she would have Googled him, but she'd long since realised that Nick had given Sorcha strict instructions not to let her anywhere near such things. It was as though he wanted her to be cocooned away from all technology, as though he believed it was somehow dangerous to him, that it might threaten his complete control of the situation. It was only Sorcha's pleading that meant they were allowed to keep the television in the apartment and that was just as well, since she seemed to spend hours watching it during her down time. Whenever Allie woke up in the dead of night, she would hear muted sounds coming from the lounge and knew that Sorcha was watching it around the clock, never ever taking time to sleep.

As for Nick, Allie hadn't really seen that much of him over the past few weeks. Oh, he'd popped up occasionally to take a quick report from Sorcha on how things were progressing, but then he'd always announce that he had other fish to fry and would walk away without even looking back. Sorcha, on the other hand, was always there, day and night. Allie had grown to like her a lot and really enjoyed her company, but just occasionally she'd have loved to be allowed a little time to herself. It was almost as though Sorcha was her prison warder, constantly keeping an eye on her charge, making sure that she didn't break the terms of her contract. Even now she was sitting sullenly in the back row, observing the rehearsal, looking bored and saying nothing.

'Okay, positions, everyone,' announced Martin. Allie went obediently to the centre of the performance space and knelt down, assuming the pose of a girl lost in a trance. Dean allowed a little time to elapse before walking slowly out behind her.

'What's the matter, girl?' he cried.

Allie reacted, twisting around to look at him in apparent dismay, and she launched into the script, thinking as she did so how much happier she was now that the script been changed into everyday English. The producers had been adamant at first that they didn't want it altered from the weird, rambling dialect Justin had originally written it in, telling her how 'exquisite' and 'poetic' the language was, how faithful to the period in which the story was set. But the truth was, Allie just couldn't handle it. She seemed to stumble over every other line, unable to get her tongue around the odd phrasing. At one point she'd even been moved to tears, protesting that she couldn't do it the way it was written and that was that. They'd just have to find somebody else for the role, somebody who understood what Justin was trying to say!

But then, out of the blue, Nick had called by one evening. He'd taken the production team off to another room for a conference, and had somehow persuaded them to accept Allie's suggestions.

'How did you convince them?' Allie asked him afterwards.

'Oh, I just assured them that it would all sound so much better if they simply threw out all those 'thees' and 'thous' and 'Faithers' and 'Mithers' and said the lines as people actually speak now.'

'And Justin went along with it?'

'He wasn't exactly happy about it. But I just looked him in the eye and explained how much better it would be; how much more successful. And after all, that's what we all want, right?'

Sure enough, the very next day, Justin had turned up with copies of a new script and had handed them out to the cast without another word.

With Nick's help, Allie had also managed to change various bits of the story she didn't much care for, including a lengthy scene where Jason's character attempted to interrogate Theresa whilst beating her mercilessly with a stick. Allie had considered the whole thing dreadfully over the top and it was very hard to act being in pain, so she'd mentioned it to Nick the next time she saw him, and sure enough, that scene too had been promptly rewritten. In the new version, the priest was much more considerate of her, confining himself simply to asking searching questions. And now Allie was beginning to understand how this process worked – that through Nick, she could shape the play to suit her own preferences. It was simply a question of asking.

Now, as she launched into the dialogue she'd been through so many times already, it occurred to her that something else still didn't feel right.

'Father, I had a vision. I saw a man dressed in white and he told me…' Allie stopped, shook her head and turned to look at Martin. 'I'm sorry,' she said. 'This isn't working.'

Martin sighed wearily. Dean let out a groan and rolled his eyes. It wasn't the first time this had happened. There were dark mutterings from the other actors waiting at the side of the space for their cues. 'All right, everybody,' said Martin, waving his hands in an attempt to quell the rumblings of discontent. 'Let's take a ten minute break.'

There were some incredulous looks and more grumbling before the other actors trooped out of the room, leaving Allie alone with Martin and Justin. Sorcha looked from Allie to Martin as though challenging the idea that she should leave too, but a caustic glare from Martin confirmed that he wanted her out of there, so she got up from her seat and slouched after the others, slamming the door loudly behind her. Allie got up from the floor and walked across to Martin and Justin.

'Allie, I'm not being funny,' said Martin, 'but we've only a few days to go before we perform this and all these interruptions really aren't helping.'

'I know that,' said Allie. 'But I just don't feel right saying that line. "I saw a man dressed in white." I mean, I'm supposed to have seen an extraterrestrial, aren't I? So surely it would be somebody dressed in silver or glowing from within or whatever?'

Martin looked to Justin for help.

'That's just the way her fifteenth century mindset is seeking to explain the situation,' said Justin. 'She's trying to put it into the kind of terms her own brain can understand.'

'What, so she'd get mixed up about a colour?' Allie shook her head. 'That doesn't make any sense.'

Justin appeared to be close to losing his temper. 'Look,' he said, 'I've gone a long way to try to accommodate your ideas, Allie. For goodness' sake, I've already changed half of the dialogue! You and Nick have massacred the play. I barely recognise it as the piece I wrote. And now, I'm honestly beginning to wonder whose work this actually is. Don't forget, I'm the playwright here. I'm the one who won the competition, so...'

The door opened and a familiar figure strolled into the room. He walked straight to an empty seat and sat himself down.

'Ah, Nick,' said Martin, warily. 'How nice of you to join us. We were just discussing the script. A small point that Allie isn't happy with.'

'Oh yes?' said Nick, smiling that bright, dangerous smile of his. He turned his gaze to look at Justin and Allie could see the look of apprehension in the playwright's eyes as he squirmed under that basilisk stare. 'What seems to be the problem?' asked Nick quietly.

'Oh well, she's quibbling about a word, to be honest,' said Justin. 'It says "white" in the script and she wants to say "silver" instead. I was just pointing out to her that somebody at that time would...'

'It doesn't seem such a terrible request to me,' observed Nick. 'One word. That's not exactly a big deal, is it?'

'Well, no, but...'

'So, surely, if that's all Allie wants, we can accommodate that, can't we?'

Justin seemed to bristle for a moment. 'It just seems to me that this is my play and I...'

'And it seems to me,' replied Nick, 'that I've arranged for this production to have certain things that weren't in the original brief. A superior lighting rig, for instance. A top quality sound technician. And when you wanted the services of established actors and a celebrated director...' He waved a hand at Martin. '... who was it who came up with the budget?'

Justin nodded. 'I understand that. And, please don't think that I'm not grateful for all your help, but...'

Nick concentrated his gaze. 'Don't you want to stay in my good books?' he asked. 'Hmm?'

'Well, of course I do, but, you can surely see–'

'See what?'

'That what you are doing just isn't fair. Between the two of you, you're ruining my play!'

'Your play?' Nick did something then, something with his right hand. He clenched it into a fist and squeezed tightly. Justin stopped talking abruptly. His eyes bulged and he caught his breath. His face turned a ghastly shade of white. He opened his mouth to say something but all that emerged was a gasp. Then his eyes filled with blood. Two red trails began to trickle down his face. Allie stared at him, wanting to do something to help him, but somehow she felt incapable of moving so much as a muscle. There was a long, horrible silence. Finally, Nick relaxed his grip and Justin's shoulders jerked. He let out a desperate breath and sat slumped in his chair, staring dully back at Nick.

'Make the change,' snarled Nick, and after a few moments, Justin averted his gaze and nodded meekly. He wiped at his eyes with the back of his sleeve, smearing trails of blood across his pale face.

'Excellent,' said Nick, as though he considered the matter dealt with. 'Now, if you two gentlemen wouldn't mind making yourselves scarce for ten minutes, I need a quick consultation with our star.'

Martin looked for a moment as though he too might be considering an objection, but he must have thought better of it, because he turned on his heel and left the room. After a few moments' hesitation, Justin got up from his seat and trudged wearily after him. Nick waited until they'd closed the door, then gestured to Allie to come and sit beside him. She did as he wanted, but looked up at him uncertainly.

'What did you just do?' she asked him.

'It's called negotiation,' he said calmly.

'But he... his eyes...'

'Yes, he really should see a specialist about that,' said Nick. 'Could be storing up a whole host of problems for the future.' He looked at her intently. 'So,' he purred. 'How is everything?'

Allie shrugged. 'OK, I suppose.'

'Just OK?' Nick looked disappointed. 'Aren't you enjoying preparing for your first role? I thought you'd be excited.'

'Well, it's not really what I expected,' said Allie. 'I...'

'Go on.'

'Well, I don't want to sound ungrateful, but I'm not mad about Justin's play. To my mind, it's a bit... weird.'

'Weird?' His expression suggested he was unfamiliar with the word. 'Allie, this is a prizewinning piece.'

'Yes, but I was hoping for something a bit more fun. You know, *Grease*? *Legally Blonde*. Something like that.'

'Hmm.' Nick seemed to consider this for a moment. 'Well, to be honest, Allie, you don't have to love the play. It is, after all, simply a step in the right direction. And let me remind you that The Traverse has an extraordinary reputation. There are young actors out there that would give their right arms for an opportunity to appear here.'

'I appreciate that, but...'

133

'And the great reviews you get for this role will secure you something more mainstream, further down the line, you can depend on that.'

'If it gets great reviews,' muttered Allie, unconvinced.

'Oh, I'm confident that it will,' said Nick. 'Once they see the calibre of your performance.' He reached into his inside pocket and pulled out some sheets of paper. 'Here, these may serve to cheer you up a bit,' he said.

Allie took the sheets and peered at them dubiously. They seemed to comprise a list of typed names and a list of publications, some of which she hadn't heard of – but most of which she undoubtedly had. *The Guardian*, *The Telegraph*, *The Independent*, *The Scottish Evening Post*. 'What are these exactly?' she asked.

'That's a list of the publications who are sending reviewers on the opening night,' he said.

'The opening night for what?' she exclaimed. It began to dawn on her, slowly and horribly. 'The opening night for *Rapture*?' she croaked.

'Well, yes, obviously, *Rapture*! Why would I show you a list of reviewers for another production?'

'But...' She scanned the sheet again. 'These people won't come out to see somebody like me!'

'I think you'll find they will,' said Nick, calmly. 'I seem to have to keep reminding you that The Traverse is the most respected theatre in Scotland for new writing. Of course all the papers will be there for your moment of triumph.'

'But, they'll slaughter us!'

'That would be a memorable first night,' said Nick, almost wistfully. 'But relax, I'm sure they'll love the show. You just have to demonstrate to them what you can do. I think they'll appreciate your talents.'

Allie scowled. 'You say that, but you don't know. You haven't even seen me act!'

'Nonsense! I saw your audition, didn't I? It was remarkable.'

'Yes, but that's not quite the same thing. I mean, you're taking it on trust that I can do it. When I think about it, even I'm not sure that I can!'

'That's silly. What about Miss Marston? She believed in you.'

'It's Miss Marchmont!' Allie corrected him. 'And maybe she was just being nice. Now all these big name critics are coming to see me. They'll probably think I'm terrible! They'll crucify me!'

'Now, now…' Nick reached out a hand and placed it on Allie's shoulder. Immediately, she felt that familiar sense of calm settling over her. 'Allie, I have the greatest faith in you. I know what you're capable of and I intend to show that to the world. Now stop getting yourself all hot and bothered, because I have some interesting news for you.'

'You do?'

'Oh yes. I'm sure you can't have failed to notice that only a short distance away from here there's another theatre. An older one. The Royal Lyceum.'

'Of course I've noticed,' said Allie, fully calm now, almost relaxed. 'They're showing *A Midsummer Night's Dream* at the moment. I was hoping I might get to see it some time, but Martin won't even let me have a night off.'

'Oh, you leave Martin to me,' suggested Nick. 'I'm sure one night's relaxation won't harm your performance in the slightest.' He looked puzzled. 'Anyway, I thought you preferred musicals.'

'I like things I can understand,' she assured him. 'And of course I've studied Shakespeare. I'm not a complete ignoramus.'

'I'm sure you're not.' He smiled. 'Anyway, it's not the Lyceum's current show I wanted to talk about. It's their next. I wonder, Allie, if you have any idea what it's going to be?'

Allie shook her head. 'Haven't a clue,' she said.

Nick's smile deepened. 'A little bird told me that it's going to be Arthur Miller's *The Crucible.*'

Allie's eyes widened. She stared at him. 'No way,' she said.

'Way,' he assured her. 'They've just started rehearsals.'

'Oh.' Allie couldn't help but feel crushed. 'Then I suppose, they must have already cast it.'

'Yes, I'm afraid so. I understand somebody called Roxanne Walsh is playing Abigail…'

'Roxanne Walsh? You're kidding me!'

'No, not at all.' He looked thoughtful. 'Oh yes, I remember you mentioning her to me the night we met.'

'That's right.' Allie stared at him. 'She's fantastic. She's kind of like my hero, you know? My absolute favourite actor in the world.' She thought for a moment. 'It's weird her playing that role, though. Abigail's just a kid, Roxanne will be way too old for it. Still, I bet she'll pull it off. If anyone can do it, she can.'

'Hmm. Well, anyway, I just wanted to say that I'll be able to organise some free tickets for you when it's on,' said Nick. ' Since you like her so much.'

'Are you sure you can't get me a role in it?' murmured Allie.

He shook his head. 'Sorry, but as I said, it's already cast, apart from a few smaller roles. You wouldn't be interested in those. No, we need to find something bigger and brasher for you. Something where you can sing and dance – take the lead role.'

'No, wait. If it meant I could work with Roxanne Walsh, then maybe I could take a smaller part.'

Nick looked doubtful. 'But that would be a step down, Allie. You have equal billing in *Rapture*. You hardly want to throw that aside for a walk-on.'

'Yes, but it's Roxanne Walsh. And I'd love to work with her. I could learn so much from her.'

Nick frowned. 'I'm not sure. Let me have a think about it. After all the accolades you'll get for this production, you could probably walk in to any major role you fancy.'

Allie snorted. 'You don't know that we're going to get good reviews for *Rapture*. What if they hate me?'

Nick lifted a hand to stroke her face. 'How could they hate you, Allie? They just have to look at you to know how special you really are.'

Again she felt something envelope her, a curious, soothing warmth and in an instant all her anxiety seemed to evaporate. 'Do you really mean that?' she whispered.

'Of course I do. I knew from the moment I met you that you had great potential and that I only needed to unlock it. So trust me. Everything is going to be fine.' He lowered his hand. 'Now,' said Nick, getting back to his feet. 'Let's call the others back in, shall we? Time waits for no-one.'

'Can't you stay and watch a while?' she asked him, hopefully.

He sighed, shook his head. 'I'd love to,' he said. 'There's nothing I'd like more. Unfortunately…' He glanced at the back of his wrist, which was ridiculous since he made a point of never wearing a watch. 'Unfortunately, I have to be somewhere else right now. Busy, busy, busy. But don't worry, I have complete faith in you.' He gave her shoulder a last pat and then walked towards the door. 'I'll summon the others, shall I?' he asked without turning his head.

'Sure,' she replied and watched as he went out through the door. A few moments later, the others trudged back in, looking wary. Justin slunk meekly to his seat, Sorcha took her place at the back and the other actors moved to their starting positions. Allie walked to the centre of the performance space and knelt down.

Martin appraised the room for a moment, waiting until everyone was in position. 'Right,' he said. 'Let's take it from the top, shall we?'

16

OPENING NIGHT

Allie woke with the dull ache of anxiety coiling and squirming in the pit of her stomach. She'd had a terrible night's sleep, haunted by dreams in which she saw herself standing on a huge stage, tongue-tied and clumsy in front of a gawping, silent crowd. She was thankful that something had woken her. She blinked several times to clear her eyes and realised that Sorcha had just opened the blinds to allow the morning sunlight into the bedroom. Now she was bringing over a tray filled with breakfast things.

'Good morning, good morning, good morning!' she trilled, in that fake gleeful tone she had taken to using lately, a technique that completely failed to mask her inner misery. 'It's your big day, sweetie. Did you sleep OK?'

'No, not at all,' complained Allie, struggling wearily into a sitting position. 'I had nightmares. Awful nightmares.' She contemplated the tray without enthusiasm. 'I can't eat that,' she said. 'I'm way too nervous.'

'Don't be daft. You'll be fine! And I've got all your favourites here. Softly-boiled eggs. Marmite soldiers. You've got to keep your strength up.' She set the tray carefully down on Allie's lap. 'Go on, you must have something.'

Allie picked up the coffee mug and took a cautious sip. 'It's going to be a total disaster,' she said bleakly. 'I won't remember my lines. I'll look stupid.' She noticed a white envelope propped up beside her rack of buttered toast. 'What's this?' she asked, picking it up.

'Search me,' said Sorcha, settling herself on the end of the bed. 'It dropped through the letterbox a few minutes ago. I suppose it's a letter.'

'A letter?' Allie grimaced. 'Who even writes letters?' She turned over the envelope and instantly recognised the neat loops and crosses of the handwriting. 'Oh shit,' she said. 'It's from my mum.'

Sorcha sat up and looked interested. 'Really? Wow. That's quite a big deal, right?' She studied Allie's troubled face for a while and then asked impatiently. 'Well, aren't you going to open it?'

Allie shrugged. 'I don't know if I should,' she muttered. 'She'll probably be going off on one. Knowing her, she'll have set the police on me – the child welfare association, something like that.'

There was a short silence. 'There's only one way to find out,' suggested Sorcha, and Allie could see that she had a point. She'd have to face the music sooner or later. She'd barely even thought about her parents since she'd arrived here. Now they had finally got in touch. She fully expected the letter to be full of veiled threats and desperate entreaties for Allie to come home, but as it turned out, it wasn't like that at all.

Dear Allie

I hope you don't mind me writing to you like this, but Nick explained to us how you don't have access to a phone or a computer now and I didn't want to just turn up at your apartment out of the blue.

Of course, your dad and I were out of our minds when you disappeared the way you did and naturally we contacted the police and told them all about the situation. (I hope you won't be angry about that, but we were so worried!) But then, the very next day, Nick turned up on our doorstep and explained everything! I'll admit we were very dubious at first, (especially your dad!) but when he told us about all the famous actors he'd already discovered over the years, Nick set both our minds at rest. And when he showed us the brochure for your new apartment in Edinburgh, well, it looks like a dream home! And now you're already starring in your very first play!

We're both incredibly proud and excited for you and naturally we'll be there on your opening night to give you our support – not that it sounds like you'll need it, from what Nick's been telling us. He's organised a chauffeur-driven limousine for the opening night and even booked us into a fancy restaurant for dinner – at his expense, mind! I hope you'll find time to join us afterwards for a wee bite to eat, but of course, we'll understand if you're too busy.

I won't say 'good luck' as I know you theatrical types are funny about that kind of thing. Instead, I'll just say 'break a leg!!!' but I know that you'll be wonderful in the role. See you soon.

Love

Mum xxxxx

Allie shook her head and groaned. She handed the letter to Sorcha and, picking up a slice of toast from the tray, she nibbled at it distractedly.

Sorcha scanned the letter quickly and then looked at Allie. 'She seems OK with the idea,' she observed.

'Yeah. That's the problem. I really don't get it. I thought she'd be mad at me. I thought…'

'Nick will have charmed her,' said Sorcha. 'He's good at that.'

'Over the years,' murmured Allie.

'Come again?'

Allie patted the letter with one finger. 'Mum says "all the big stars he's discovered over the years." But why would she say that about a man who is only a few years older than me? '

Sorcha looked evasive. 'Well,' she began, 'maybe…'

'Because he looks much older to Mum, right? And of course, why wouldn't he? He'd want to be the right age to charm her, wouldn't he? Because that's how it works, isn't it Sorcha? He looks different to everybody he meets.' She thought for a moment. 'How old does he look to you?'

'To me? Well,'

'Go on, tell me the truth.'

Sorcha let out a sigh. 'I suppose he looks about my age,' she said.

Allie sighed. She dropped the slice of nibbled toast back onto the plate. 'That's obviously how he does it,' she said. 'He lets people see what they want to see.' She thought for a moment and then gasped. 'The guy who showed us this apartment. He thought Nick was my father!' She looked at Sorcha. 'So how old is he really?'

Sorcha looked uncomfortable. 'I really couldn't say,' she replied. 'He's clocked up a few miles, I guess.' She waved a hand at Allie's plate. 'Look, you don't want to be bothering yourself with all that stuff,' she said. 'You really should eat a bit more. You've a big day ahead of you.'

'I can't,' said Allie, pushing the tray away. 'You eat it.'

'Oh, I've already had something,' said Sorcha, dismissively.

Allie felt a sense of irritation rising within her. 'No you haven't,' she said. 'Don't lie to me; I hate it when you do that.'

'Allie, I...'

'Come to think of it, I don't think I've ever seen you eat anything. Not so much as a crumb.'

'Don't be silly,' said Sorcha. 'Of course I eat! I... usually have something after you've gone to bed.'

'But you don't!' protested Allie. 'All you ever have is sauvignon blanc, which trust me, does not count as one of your five a day.'

'It's got grapes in it,' said Sorcha, trying to break Allie's chain of thought.

'No, I'm not letting you wriggle out of this,' insisted Allie. 'It's only me who ever eats anything in this place.' She stared at Sorcha. 'But that's doesn't make any sense, because if a person doesn't eat, eventually they'd...' She broke off as a terrible thought occurred to her. 'Oh God, Sorcha, that's not it, is it?'

'Don't talk crazy,' muttered Sorcha.

'No, I'm serious. You–' She shook her head, not wanting to even consider the idea, but the reality was right there in front of her and it didn't help that Sorcha couldn't seem to look her in the eye. Allie reached out and took hold of Sorcha's wrist, noting as she did so how horribly cold it felt to the touch. 'Sorcha, tell me the truth, now. Are you...?'

Again, she broke off, because even saying it would make her sound crazy. 'I remember you told me... you said that the first time you met Nick was when you were thinking about jumping off that bridge and he came along and talked you out of it.' She broke off again as something happened she'd never seen before. Sorcha's kohl-ringed eyes were brimming with tears, making ugly black trails down her white face. 'No,' said Allie, shaking her head. 'Oh no, that can't be it. It can't!'

'But it is,' wailed Sorcha. 'Don't you see? It's very simple, Allie. Nick didn't get to me till after I jumped. He got to me when I was already regretting what I'd done and the two of us, we... we cut a deal.'

'I thought you said you didn't sign a contract?'

'I didn't. Once you've ended things, you're not entitled to very much at all. You can just... agree to work for Nick... as an assistant. You're there whenever he needs you for something. It's not life, exactly, but it sometimes feels a little bit like it.' She wiped her eyes on the back of her arm, spreading the trails of kohl in all directions. 'I thought it would be better than, you know, the alternative. But I didn't realise then that it would go on forever.'

Allie could hardly breathe now. She was trying to accept what she'd just been told but her brain couldn't seem to compute it.

'Sorcha, how long have you been working for him?'

Sorcha sniffed, shook her head. 'A very long time,' she said.

'But your fashion—' Allie waved a hand at her companion. 'That can't have been before, say, the nineteen-nineties?'

Sorcha laughed bitterly. 'I haven't always looked like this, sweetie. I've changed my look over the years, lots of times – hundreds of times. Back when I stepped out onto that bridge, we were all wearing crinolines and bonnets. That really sucked.'

Allie was desperately trying to think of some kind of

plan. 'So... I mean, well, there surely must come a time when you've finally paid back your debt, right? There has to come a day when he sets you free.'

'I don't think so. I think he's got me forever.'

'And are there others in your position?'

Now Sorcha actually managed a chuckle. 'Sweetie, there are millions of us, all over the planet. Hey, what do you think? Maybe we should form a union!' But then she was crying again and Allie could do nothing but hold Sorcha in her arms while she sobbed, all the while aware of the icy chill seeping through her torn black T-shirt.

Allie stood in the wings and waited for her cue. Her heart was beating like a sledgehammer in her chest, her mouth was parched and she could hardly breathe, she was so scared.

The day had drifted eerily by in a kind of haze and, looking back, it was like some protracted dream that she couldn't quite wake up from. It had all happened like clockwork. The short walk to the theatre. Seeing the hastily photocopied 'Sold Out' notices stuck onto all the posters in the foyer. The final run-through with Martin and the cast. Getting herself into costume and then the slow, maddening application of makeup. The minutes ticking furiously by, going far too quickly for comfort, with Allie wishing she could stop time altogether, to give herself a chance to come to terms with what was going to happen. She was about to make her debut on the freaking stage! And not the stage of a school hall. One of the most respected theatres in Edinburgh. Her most deeply desired ambition was about to come true. She didn't know whether to laugh or cry or scream, or just head for the exit and run.

Then, all too soon, it was time to take her position in the

wings, listening in silent dread to the buzz of the audience as they filed into the theatre and settled themselves into their seats. Thoughts churned and hammered through her head, things she didn't want to remind herself of, but somehow couldn't stop. There were professional critics in the audience tonight, people who could slay her ambitions with a few malicious taps on a keyboard. The show was already sold out for its entire short run and the theatre were considering adding extra dates to avoid disappointing all the people who'd tried to buy tickets.

'Unprecedented,' somebody in the box office had told her on her way in. What's more, her parents were in the audience tonight! Jesus, the thought of them sitting out there watching her perform gave her the chills. And it wasn't just them. A short while ago, a stagehand had come to the dressing room and handed her a scribbled note. Miss Marchmont was here! Somehow, she'd found out about her ex-pupil's success and had come along to show her support. Allie didn't know whether to be delighted or mortified. Miss Marchmont, the woman who had first ignited this crazy dream, would be here to see if Allie really did have what it took to be an actor.

Oh yes, and there was one more thing; a thought that had nothing to do with tonight but kept rattling unbidden through her head just the same. Sorcha, her newly acquired friend and assistant, was dead. She'd killed herself many years ago, yet when Allie lifted her head and looked deeper into the wings, there she stood, half-hidden in shadows, smiling at Allie and giving her an encouraging thumbs-up.

And now the house lights were going down and the introductory music was playing and Allie would be on stage in just a few seconds and she couldn't even remember her first bloody line! The dream she'd had the previous night came back to haunt her, the dream of standing tongue-tied on a stage while an unseen audience watched in aching silence. She couldn't bear such humiliation. She'd rather die than endure that!

The music gave a last strident blare and faded away altogether. It was time. It was time to go on; she couldn't delay a moment longer. But she couldn't move a muscle! She was lost. In the silence, she could imagine the audience sitting out there, filled with expectation, waiting for something extraordinary to happen, something good, something exciting! They would be disappointed. They would watch in stunned silence as she fluffed her lines and bumped into the scenery. This was going to be horrible.

She snatched in a deep breath and walked out onto the stage, aware of her own footsteps clumping loudly on the wooden boards.

And somehow, the opening line came to her. She opened her mouth and heard her own voice – a pathetic, wheedling noise that sounded ridiculous in the silence, uttering the first line. Somehow, she managed to convince it to keep going, to say the next line and then the next and, after what seemed an eternity, Dean strode onto the stage and the two of them exchanged lines. His voice was steady, powerful, totally convincing. Beside him, she sounded like an idiot, a squawking child desperately striving for attention, but she willed herself to keep going, hoping that soon she'd get into the swing of it, that she'd start to believe what her own voice was saying, that she'd find the character she was supposed to be inhabiting – but that feeling never came.

It was a straight run – ninety minutes, no interval, and as the play neared its end, she was soaked in a chill, clammy sweat, her voice a pitiful croak in her flayed throat and she told herself that once this was over, she would leave the theatre, she would run back to her apartment and cry herself to sleep. And she would never again make the mistake of thinking she could act.

She spoke the final line of text and stood, staring out into the unseen audience. The lights faded, went slowly down into darkness. There was a silence so deep she thought she could hear her own heart beating. It was over and she had failed dismally.

And then the applause began. It started hesitantly, some people unsure that the play was actually over, but it built quickly in volume, louder, louder. Then the lights came back on and Allie stared around in disbelief because as far as she could see, every single person in the audience was standing up and now they were cheering and whistling and stamping their feet. She saw the looks of astonished delight on the faces of her fellow actors and then everybody moved to the front of the stage, linked hands and bowed. They left the stage and went into the wings, but the applause didn't abate, if anything it grew in volume, so they hurried back, took another bow and then another, before Dean looked at everyone and said, 'That's enough,' but even as they walked off for the final time, it was with the sound of the crowd echoing in their ears.

Sorcha hurried forward and gave Allie an enthusiastic hug. 'You were brilliant!' she said, but Allie couldn't make herself believe it. She freed herself from Sorcha's icy embrace and sneaked back to the side of the stage, so she could peek out through a narrow gap in the curtains and gaze down into the packed seats. It took a little while to locate him, but finally she did, the only person still sitting. He was towards the back of the theatre, directly behind Allie's parents, and she saw too that he was the only person not applauding. He was just sitting there, gazing towards the empty stage, a curious half smile on his lips. As she watched, he finally stood up and it was as though somebody had flicked a switch. The audience stopped applauding and now they were turning to look at each other with dazed expressions, as though wondering why their hands were stinging from the effort of clapping them so furiously together. Allie saw that Nick was speaking to her parents and she noted how they hung on to every word he said, nodding enthusiastically, laughing with him, Mum leaning forward as though entranced by his every utterance.

Allie was aware of a chill presence beside her and she saw that Sorcha was there, looking through the same gap in the curtains.

'He did this,' said Allie quietly. 'He made them like me.'

'Aw, no,' said Sorcha. 'It was you, sweetie, nobody else. You were great.'

But Allie had already turned away and was striding back to the dressing room, her eyes filling with tears.

17

A CELEBRATION

They were back in the Forth Floor Brasserie and Allie was beginning to wonder why she'd ever agreed to come along. Her parents sat across the table from her, beaming at her in a most disconcerting fashion, as though she were the most amazing thing in the entire room, as though they were incredibly proud to be seen in her presence. To her right sat Sorcha, glumly contemplating a plate of food but making no attempt to eat any of it. And to her left was Nick, presiding over this little post-show celebration in his own inimitable style. Right now, he was charging up some glasses with champagne, a bottle of which had just been brought to the table by his favourite waiter. Allie's father had done some oohing and aahing about the champagne, saying that he'd heard this was a really fine vintage and Nick had assured him that he'd have a crate of it sent to him first thing tomorrow.

'You'd better get used to the taste,' he told Dad, with a sly wink. 'I predict this will be the first of many.' He lowered his voice as though to confide a secret. 'You know, as it's a special occasion, I think we might allow Allie to have one wee glass of bubbly? What do you say, Roger?'

Dad considered for a moment and then nodded. 'I believe that would be in order,' he said and Nick handed everybody a glass. 'To Allie,' he said and raised his drink.

Dad, Mum and Sorcha followed suit. They all took a gulp, savoured the taste and then set their glasses down.

'Oh Allie, I'm so glad you decided to come along!' trilled Mum. 'What a wonderful evening! I'm so proud, I could burst.'

'I wouldn't if I were you,' said Allie, quietly. 'It would make a terrible mess of the upholstery.'

Mum stared at her blankly for a moment and then laughed, a little too loudly. She looked at her husband for support. 'Wasn't it brilliant, Roger?'

Dad nodded enthusiastically. 'It was exceptional,' he said. 'Allie, I had no idea you were so talented.'

Allie lifted her own glass and drained its contents in one gulp. She fixed her father with a cool look. 'What was so great about it?' she asked him.

'Er... well, everything,' he said. 'You particularly, of course, but... the story, the other actors, umm...' He looked at Mum as if seeking help.

'The music?' she suggested.

'Yes, Margaret, that too! Very atmospheric. It took me right into that world. Of course, you were the stand-out, Allie, but it really was a fabulous piece all round.' He glanced at Nick. 'It's wonderful to see that my daughter has fallen in with such a good influence.'

Allie laughed bitterly at that. She couldn't stop herself. She waved her empty glass at Nick. He shook his head, so she reached out, took the bottle from the ice bucket and topped herself up, ignoring his outraged expression. 'What about your big plans for me?' she asked her father. 'Eh? Exams? University? I thought that was the path you wanted for me.'

Dad smiled ruefully. 'Well, I'll admit, we thought it was the right way to go, at the time. And we weren't at all sure about this acting lark. But Nick has assured us that you can make a success of it and my goodness, I think you'll agree, he's certainly got you off to an excellent start! Why, I've read that most actors have to spend years struggling along in bit parts before they ever make anything of themselves, but he's somehow managed to put you straight into a lead role.'

'Not the lead role, Roger,' Nick corrected him. 'At least, not officially. The Traverse are very insistent on that point. The performers are given equal billing.' He gave Allie a sly look. 'But it's certainly what you would call a pivotal role.'

'Absolutely. Pivotal. That's exactly right.' Dad lifted his glass to Nick. 'I have to hand it to you,' he said. 'You seem to know exactly what you're doing.'

Nick waved a hand in dismissal. 'It's all down to Allie's natural talent,' he assured them. 'I've merely been able to... steer her a little.' He lowered his voice slightly and glanced quickly around as if to assure himself he was not being overheard. 'Of course, I won't consider my work properly done until Allie has a proper lead role. But, all in good time. Today I have managed to secure her an audition for something new. Something she actually asked me for.'

'Oh yes,' said Dad. 'What's that, then?'

'It's for the Royal Lyceum's next production,' said Nick. '*The Crucible.*'

'*The Crucible*!' exclaimed Dad as though it was the most amazing thing he'd ever heard. 'But that's–'

'Exactly,' said Nick. 'The play she loves more than any other. The one she was born to be in. It's only a small role, of course, but one that I feel will be a very useful step on her way to the top.'

'The Lyceum!' sighed Mum. 'Everyone in Scotland has

heard of the Lyceum. Oh, Allie, you've really landed on your feet, haven't you?'

Allie stared across the table at her parents and wondered how they could have been taken in so completely. But then, she reminded herself, she had been taken in too, just as effortlessly. It was only now that she was beginning to realise that things weren't quite as rosy as they had initially seemed.

'And wasn't it lovely to see Miss Marchmont at the theatre!' exclaimed Mum, remembering. 'We had a quick word with her in the foyer. Did she manage to find her way backstage to you, Allie?'

Allie nodded, remembering how her former teacher had appeared in the doorway of the dressing room, shortly after the show's conclusion. Miss Marchmont had been babbling about how wonderful Allie's performance was, but something in her demeanour didn't quite add up. Allie could see confusion in the woman's eyes, as though she actually wanted to say something quite different to the accolades that kept spilling automatically from her mouth.

'Any criticisms?' Allie had asked her, knowing that, back at school, Miss Marchmont had always been ready to impart little bits of advice about how things might be improved, but apparently, not tonight.

'You were–' There was a long pause as Miss Marchmont tried to shape her lips around a different word to the one that eventually emerged. 'N-n-n-wonderful!' she said. 'C-c-c-Magnificent. B-b-b-Incredible.'

'Well, er, thank you,' was all that Allie could say to that. 'And thanks for coming all this way to see me.' They made a bit of small talk then about what might be the school's next production and Allie had said that yes, she'd be delighted to come back and talk to some of the pupils in next year's drama class. Then she'd watched in appalled fascination as Miss Marchmont stumbled out of the room, still looking as though an entirely different opinion was struggling to find a way from her brain to her mouth. Allie wondered if the same process had been applied to her parents. It wasn't like them to be so full of praise. They'd always been so critical of her love of drama – had warned her she'd be unemployable if she went down that road. They hadn't even wanted her to take it as an exam. Now they were acting like the founding members of the Allie Lawrence fan club.

Mum had turned her attention to Sorcha who was still staring glumly at her plate. 'Are you not very hungry, my dear?' she asked. 'The food here is absolutely delicious, you know.'

Sorcha looked up in surprise. 'Oh, I, I'm really not,' she said. 'Sorry, Mrs Lawrence, I don't–'

'She never eats,' said Allie flatly. 'She's dead, you see, and the dead have absolutely no appetite whatsoever.' She smiled at Mum, then stared challengingly along the table at Nick, who returned her gaze with cool detachment.

'I suppose that must be what's called theatrical humour,' he said. 'Allie already seems to be getting into the swing of it.' He reached out and took her half empty glass from her hand. 'Perhaps we'd better ease off on the bubbly, eh? You've another performance tomorrow.'

'Yes,' she said. 'I wonder if this one will be as well received as tonight's. Or are you not actually planning to be there?'

'It doesn't matter if I'm there or not,' he told her. 'You're the one they're coming to see.'

'Yes, but what do they see, Nick? Only what you allow them to.'

154

There was an uncomfortable silence then, over which the sounds of the restaurant's other customers seemed to rise in an unruly hubbub. Nick glanced quickly around the table. 'I wonder if you would excuse us for a moment?' he asked. 'I'd like a few words with Allie in private. About tomorrow's show.'

'No problem at all,' said Dad, who was currently topping Mum's glass up with champagne.

Allie got to her feet and followed Nick across the crowded room, to a quiet corner looking out onto St. Andrew Square. He stood for a moment, gazing out of the window, and then turned slowly to look at her, a half smile on his lips. 'Is something wrong?' he asked her, a look of complete innocence on his face. 'You don't seem entirely happy with the way things are going.'

'What could possibly be wrong?' she asked him. 'Well, let me see now. I'm appearing in a play in which everybody thinks I'm brilliant. Only problem is, I know I wasn't very good. It's the first time I've done anything on a proper stage and I struggled to get through it. How could I be any good? But even so, I somehow managed to get a standing ovation!'

Nick spread his hands. 'I'm failing to see the problem,' he told her.

'You know perfectly well what I'm saying. They're only reacting like that because you're making it happen.'

Now he looked puzzled. 'And how would I do that, exactly?'

'Oh, don't act the innocent with me! You're – I don't know, casting a spell on them or something – making them see what isn't really there.'

Nick shrugged. 'I'll admit that my presence in the audience tonight may have influenced things a bit.

Sometimes I just can't help myself. But think about this for a moment. I won't be there tomorrow, will I? I won't be there for the rest of the run. So, it's up to you now, Allie. I've engineered a really good start to your acting career. Now you will have to take it the rest of the way on your own. What do you think? Are you up to the challenge?'

She frowned. 'Seriously? From here on in, I do it myself?'

'Of course.' He reached out a hand and placed it on her shoulder, and once again she felt that sensual glow pulsing through her. 'All right, I suppose I might be guilty of smoothing your path into this a little bit. Sometimes I just can't help myself. And you can't blame me, surely? At the end of the day, I only want the very best for you.'

Allie could feel her resentment melting away and she was somehow powerless to hang onto it. 'What about Sorcha?' she asked.

'What about her?' asked Nick, and his expression turned abruptly back into a mask of disdain. 'What has she been saying to you?'

'Nothing. She didn't say anything. I kind of worked it out for myself. About how she is–'

'If she's disappointed you in some way, I can remove her.' Nick clicked his fingers. 'As easily as that! I can assign somebody else to be your guardian.'

'Is that what she is? My guardian?' Allie shook her head. 'Funny, I was beginning to think of her as a friend.'

Nick looked as though he was unfamiliar with the word. 'She's just an employee. She does whatever I tell her to do.'

'Well, I suppose that makes some kind of sense. And no, I don't want you to get rid of her. In fact, I really like

Sorcha. I'm kind of beginning to care about her. And after everything she's done for you, don't you think…?'

He did that thing of tilting his head to one side. 'Don't I think what?'

'That she's earned the right to rest now?'

'She has no rights,' said Nick, coldly. 'We have an understanding, the two of us. It's as simple as that.'

'And is it the same story between us? Is that how this works, Nick? Once I get that lead role you keep banging on about, that's when it's all over for me? What happens to me then?'

He shook his head. 'Oh, you don't want to worry your little head about stuff like that,' he told her. 'That's off in the future, somewhere. That could be years from now.'

Allie considered for a moment. 'Well, like you said yourself, Catherine isn't a leading role. And this thing at the Lyceum, that's just a small part, right?'

He nodded. 'Absolutely,' he said. 'You'll know when the time comes.'

'But, what if I refuse to ever take a lead role? What if I insist that I will only do walk-ons and character parts. What then?'

Nick chuckled gently. 'You're a human, Allie,' he said. 'And if there's one thing I've learned about humans, it's the fact that they are, by nature, ambitious. I've not met one yet who can resist the ultimate temptation. I don't expect you to be any different. But we'll see. I'm in no great hurry.' He glanced back into the restaurant. 'Come on,' he said. 'This is supposed to be your big night and you're missing it. Let's go back to the table.'

She sighed and nodded. For the moment all her fight had faded away. As they turned back, she saw Nick give a slight nod to the young waiter on the far side of the room and he turned and hurried away; and no sooner was Allie settling herself into her seat, than he reappeared carrying a huge cake, studded with candles and fizzing with sparklers. He set it down on the table and Allie saw her own image printed onto the icing, grinning up at her, a photograph taken during the rehearsals of *Rapture*. Underneath it was a message, written in neon red letters. *Allie Lawrence – a Star is Born!*

'Champagne for everyone!' announced Nick and suddenly every single person in the room was up from their seats and applauding wildly. Allie stared around in amazement and at that moment, she had to admit that this felt very good, better than she could ever have imagined. She knew too that she wanted more of it. What was it Nick had said? Humans were ambitious. Would she really know when it was time to put on the brakes?

But right now, despite everything he had said, Nick was pouring her one more glass of champagne. And that cake looked very tasty indeed.

18

REVIEW

'This is what *The Guardian* thought,' announced Sorcha. It was the morning after Allie's debut performance and the two girls were lying side-by-side on the bed, the breakfast tray finished with and set down on the floor. Sorcha had gone out early to the newsagent's and had returned with a copy of every newspaper she could lay her hands on. She began to read aloud.

'Rapture is a tightly constructed four-hander, written by prize-winning playwright Justin Balfour and set in an unspecified location in Ayrshire in the fifteenth century...'

'Skip that bit,' suggested Allie. 'Get to the stuff about me.' Sorcha smiled but did as she was told.

'The role of Catherine is played by newcomer, Allie Lawrence, who makes an extraordinarily affecting debut, wringing every last ounce of emotion from a challenging role and announcing to all present that here is an incredible new talent with a hugely promising future ahead of her. As the story moves towards its tragic conclusion, I literally find myself unable to take my eyes off her. There are other, more seasoned actors on that tiny stage, but I confess I barely notice them. Lawrence is a genuine phenomenon – and a future star.'

Sorcha grinned at Allie. 'I can't quite put my finger on it,' she said, 'but there's something about that review that makes me think he rather likes you.'

Allie sniggered. 'Think so?' She shook her head. 'I just wish I could believe what–' She looked at Sorcha questioningly. 'What's he called?'

'Mark Rillington,' said Sorcha obligingly.

'I just wish I could believe what Mark Rillington is saying about me.'

Sorcha indicated the litter of discarded papers on one side of the bed. On the other side, a stack of neatly folded newsprint still waited hopefully to be read. They were about halfway through the selection that Sorcha had purchased, and so far every single review had been more than just positive. 'They're all pretty much saying the same thing,' observed Sorcha. 'The sun shines out of Allie Lawrence's cute little backside. Must be nice to be so popular.'

'I'd be happier if I believed it was genuine.' Allie looked at Sorcha. 'Look, I know your instructions are to butter me up, but there's no point in pretending any more. I get how this works. Nick influenced those critics to say that stuff. I don't exactly know how he did it, but just the same, it happened. Now I have to prove myself. The tickets are all sold, there'll be an audience in every night and they aren't going to just believe what the reviews tell them. So I have to improve, don't I? And the only way to do that is to give it everything I've got.'

'That's the spirit,' said Sorcha. She lifted a hand and the two of them slapped palms in a triumphant gesture. They lay there looking at each other for a few moments.

'Tell me more,' said Allie, at last. 'About your life before you decided to... you know. You said something about a boy you fancied?'

Sorcha scowled. 'Ah, you don't want to hear about that,' she said. 'That's ancient history.'

'That's the thing,' said Allie. 'You told me a wee bit about it before but I was seeing it like it was the present day. But this must have been, when exactly? You said something before about crinolines and bonnets? So, when exactly are we talking about?'

Sorcha sighed. 'It was the eighteen hundreds,' she said, flatly. 'If you really want to know.'

Allie felt a sense of shock go through her. 'That long?' she gasped. 'Sorcha, you must be–'

'Knackered?' ventured Sorcha and the two of them laughed.

'No, I mean, you must... you must have seen some big changes.'

'Oh, you can say that again! I mean, it's really weird, I have to go wherever I'm sent, but just by chance, I ended up working back in my home town a few years ago and the place had changed beyond all recognition. Still ugly as sin, mind you, still a dump, but kind of bustling and successful.'

'You seem to hate Australia.'

'Not Australia so much as Newcastle, New South Wales. You've got to remember, kiddo, it started out as a penal colony – you know, a place that you send prisoners to? And it didn't stop being that until the 1820s. I was born there in, I think, 1864. My daddy was a coal miner and my ma was a boozer. It wasn't exactly the nicest place in the world to be a young girl growing up, but you know, you try to make the best of things. In those days, your only aspiration was to get married before you were too far into your twenties, because if that happened, you'd be left on the shelf, what everybody called an "old maid".'

'Would that have been so bad?'

'Are you kidding? It was disastrous! All any young woman ever thought about was getting herself hitched. Nothing else really mattered.' She shook her head. 'I haven't spoken about this stuff in ages,' she said. 'I expect it sounds pretty dull.'

'No, not at all. It's fascinating. Please, keep going.' Allie put a reassuring hand on Sorcha's shoulder. 'I'd like to hear more.'

'Well, OK, if you're sure.' Sorcha paused for a moment as though considering the best way to continue. 'I guess I was around eighteen years old when I met Edward. He was just a local boy, you know, but his old man was quite wealthy, owned a lot of land, some of which had profitable coalmines on it. My parents thought they'd hit the bloody jackpot when they found out about us. My ma was already working out how she'd spend the extra moolah!' She laughed bitterly, shook her head. 'Well, Edward was a good-looking boy, you know, blonde hair, blue eyes, what you'd call drop-dead gorgeous, these days. And I genuinely thought the two of us had something real going on, you know? I thought that we'd be married, have kids, the whole shebang. That's why I gave myself to him, to use the parlance of the day, because back then, that was a big thing. Nobody fooled around out of marriage. If you did, you were damned for all eternity.' She looked thoughtful for a moment, as though something had just occurred to her. 'Anyway, in the end it was all for nothing, because I found out that he'd had somebody else on the side the whole time he was going with me. Worse than that, she was one of my best mates. You've no idea how that feels.'

'Oh, I think I do,' Allie assured her. 'I had something similar.'

'Really?' Sorcha looked surprised. 'You want to tell me about it?'

'No way, we're hearing your story right now!'

Sorcha smiled. 'Well, it sounds like you know the score. I was... like, totally humiliated. Everybody was talking about me, laughing their heads off and it seemed like I couldn't go anywhere without people were giving me these knowing looks and whispering to each other. "There she is, the prize gala!" And I suppose it just got too much for me. One day I walked out to the bridge over the Hunter River. I remember it was incredibly hot that day. The cicadas were screeching and the air felt as heavy as lead all around me, pulling the sweat out of every pore. I felt like I couldn't catch my breath. I stood there looking over the railings into the polluted water and it was like I could hear a little voice inside me, whispering, 'Why don't you do it, Edith, why don't you jump?'

Allie frowned. 'Edith?' she murmured.

Sorcha looked back at her sheepishly. 'It's my real name,' she murmured. She fixed Allie with a stare. 'Don't you dare tell anybody! If you do, I'll have to kill you.'

'Don't worry, I won't. Actually, I think it's a pretty name.'

'Yeah. In a pig's eye, it is!'

'Please, go on.'

Sorcha's eyes seemed to settle on something only she could see. 'Well, I was all set to ignore those voices, just walk away from there, but it came on me all in a rush, somehow. Like a... a madness. Almost before I knew it, I was clambering up onto the railings and I didn't hesitate, you know, I just let myself go over. Then I was falling towards the water.' She shook her head. 'You imagine that it must take a long time, don't you? But it really doesn't, it's quicker than you can draw breath. I remember the impact though. It was like a big flat hand rushed up to meet me and it hit me harder than anything I'd ever experienced.' She shrugged, shook her head. 'And that was it. I was dead.'

Allie grimaced. 'What did that feel like?' she whispered.

'Like nothing,' said Sorcha. 'Like blackness, emptiness, the darkest darkness you've ever found yourself in, and me just floating in it like a pebble in treacle, helpless, unable to move a muscle or open an eye or think a thought. I don't know how long that went on for. Could have been minutes, could have been years. But then, all of a sudden, it was like this little light blinked on right in front of my eyes and I could see this handsome face looking at me. A dark-haired guy around my own age.'

'Nick?'

'Yeah, Nick. Or Donald, as he called himself back then. Oh, I didn't know who or what he was. He was just… looking at me, and I remember he said something like, "That was pretty stupid, wasn't it?" And I had to agree with him, yes, it was bloody stupid, but I couldn't speak or even nod my head in agreement. I could only see his face, shining like the moon in the night sky. And then he asked me, "Are you regretting it yet?" I couldn't answer him but I thought to myself, "Yes, you know what, I really wish I hadn't done that." And he must have been somehow able to hear me, because he came right back at me and asked, "What if I could give you a way out? Would you take it?" And I thought to myself, "Yeah, like a bloody shot." So he said, "Come and work for me, then."

'And I thought, "But who the hell are you?" and he said, "Don't be silly. You know who I am." And it was true. I did know who he was, from the very beginning, and I realised it wasn't a good idea to get involved with him, but he'd dangled this possibility in front of me like a big juicy carrot and it felt like my last chance, so of course I knew I was going to take it. And then he held out his hand and said, "Let's shake on it." And I was just about to tell him that I couldn't move a muscle when, suddenly, I was aware of my body again and I was able to reach out and take his hand and when I did, it was like this silky warmth spilled through me, properly waking me up again, making me... whole.'

Allie nodded. She knew exactly what that felt like. She got that feeling every time Nick put a hand on her.

'And then he sent me off on my first assignment. Which was this guy in America with political ambitions...' She waved a hand. 'It was such a long time ago, I'm hazy on the details. Can't even remember his name, to tell you the truth. But like I said, there've been thousands of people since then. Sometimes I'm with them for just a few days, sometimes I'm there for years. And it can be anywhere, you know? Anywhere in the world. I mean, Nick isn't just based here. He operates everywhere, all over the globe, all at the same time.'

'How does he do that?'

'I haven't the foggiest idea, but he manages it. I don't know where I'm going until I arrive there. I don't even know how I get there, I just suddenly... am. I remember being kind of pleased, this time, to find myself back on the streets of Edinburgh, but, well, that feeling never lasts long. Because I know what's going to happen to the people I'm assigned to in the end.'

Allie frowned. 'What about me, Sorcha? Do you think you'll be with me for a long time?'

Sorcha looked doubtful. 'The way things are shaping

up for you, sweetie, I'm not planning on this being a long stay at all. You're going up like a frickin' meteor! You're already on the verge of stardom, I reckon. But however long it takes, as soon as it's done, I'll be out of here and on my way to the next job.'

'And what will happen to me when it is done?'

'I really don't know,' said Sorcha.

'But you just said–'

'I know what I said! What I meant was, I know that sooner or later, you and Nick will close your deal. After that, I'm in the dark.' She caught Allie's look of disbelief and shook her head. 'No, honest, I'm not just making that up, sweetie. I never see what happens to people and Nick never tells me anything about it. I guess it's best that I don't know. I can get quite attached to some of my clients and it doesn't help to think about them being in pain or whatever.'

'Will it involve pain?'

'Like I said, I really don't know. But I'm guessing it's not pleasant.'

Allie nodded. 'And what about you, Sorcha?'

'What about me?'

'Well, forgive me, I know you try and put on a brave face, but you really don't seem very happy in your work.'

'I'm not. I'm sick and tired of it, if you want to know the truth. If Nick came to me now and said I could go back to the way I was when he first met me, I reckon I'd take him up on the offer.'

'Really?' Allie was shocked. 'But you said you were in darkness. You couldn't even move! At least now you have some sort of life.'

Sorcha laughed bitterly. 'You call this life?' she snorted. 'Looking after a bunch of suckers who've fallen for one of Nick's deals? Watching him manipulate them, making them more and more offers they can't quite resist until he's finally got them exactly where he wants them?'

Allie grimaced. 'Is that how you think of me? As a sucker?'

'Aw, no offence, sweetie, I think you totally rock, you know? But you've fallen for Nick's bait just like all the others. And you know what? I hate to see it happening to you. Because the truth is, I really like you.'

'Does anyone ever escape the terms of the contract?'

Sorcha looked thoughtful. 'I can think of one or two in all the time I've been doing this – and only because they've somehow managed to turn their backs on their dreams. But that's a very hard thing to do, Allie! I think it's part of the human condition to want to achieve your dreams. Let's face it, it's what keeps people getting up every morning – the thought that today might just be the day when something good happens, something amazing. And Nick can give you that. But you've got to get up very early in the morning indeed to outwit him.'

Allie frowned, nodded. 'I talked to him about this, just the other day,' she said. 'To meet the terms of my contract, I just have to play a lead role in a major theatre production. But, it's like I said to him, if I refuse to ever take a lead role…'

'Yeah, it's easy to say, isn't it? But then, the opportunity comes along and I've seen so many people before you, going for it, grabbing it with both hands even though they know it spells the end for 'em. It's like they somehow just can't help themselves.'

'Well,' said Allie. 'We'll have to wait and see, won't we?'

'Yeah,' said Sorcha. 'I guess we will. In the end, I'm

afraid you'll do what all the others have done. But, I really hope not.' She waved a hand as if to dismiss the conversation, then reached over the side of the bed and selected the next paper from the pile. 'Now,' she said. 'Let's see what the *Edinburgh Evening News* made of your performance, shall we?'

She thumbed through the paper and began to read aloud.

'On Thursday night on the stage of the Traverse Theatre, Edinburgh, I witnessed something absolutely extraordinary – the birth of a new star.'

19

THE READ THROUGH

Allie and Sorcha wandered in through the glass-fronted entrance of The Royal Lyceum Theatre and stood for a moment on the white marble floor of the foyer, gazing appreciatively around. 'Wow,' murmured Sorcha. 'Pretty cool, eh?'

Allie had to agree. While The Traverse had a clean, contemporary look all of its own, it had only been in its current site since the 1990s. This beautiful Victorian theatre had been here since 1883 and just seemed to exude history.

It was only a couple of weeks since Allie's triumphant appearance at The Traverse, just a short distance from here, but those events already seemed to have receded into the dim and distant past.

As she stood waiting, she thought about how she'd put everything she had into that performance, how she felt she'd improved just a little bit every night. The muted applause the cast had received on the second evening had been evidence of the fact that without Nick's help, she really did need to try a lot harder and she'd gone at it with a vengeance, rehearsing her lines with Sorcha at every opportunity, going over and over the script, dissecting it, trying it different ways, listening to Sorcha's advice whenever it was offered. The last couple of shows (the run had been extended by several days due to unprecedented ticket demand) had felt much more accomplished than her first unaided attempts and the applause had certainly been more enthusiastic. If only she'd had another week to work on that performance, she told herself, she'd probably have actually been worth the price of admission. On the final night, there'd been a wrap party where the other members of the cast had given her their muted congratulations and had sworn they'd stay in touch (though Allie was pretty sure they wouldn't). Justin had trotted over to her and thanked her for her 'valuable input' into his script, even though his eyes had burned with a fierce resentment as he said it. Then he'd trudged morosely away into the night and Allie told herself that it would probably be the last she'd ever see of him, although she was sure he had a bright future as a playwright ahead of him.

A few days later, she'd auditioned for *The Crucible* and, true to form, Nick had managed to show up that morning, waiting out in the theatre foyer as she went through her routine for the director, David Grimes, and his two assistants. Boldly, she'd chosen to do her Abigail Williams showpiece, performing as always without a script and she knew from the 'rabbit in the headlights' stare she got from David that he was hooked, that she would certainly be offered the minor role she was after, playing Susanna Walcott, one of the girls who followed Abigail around. It would be a big step down from *Rapture*, of course – she would only have a few lines to say – but this was a big production and it was an opportunity to work alongside her acting idol, so of course she'd said yes.

Now it was the first day of rehearsals and here she was, attending the first read-through of the script. David Grimes famously advocated a holistic approach to theatre and had made it clear that he wanted everyone involved to attend from the very start.

A skinny young man wearing red-framed glasses and carrying a clipboard wandered into the foyer and gave Allie a quizzical look, so she introduced herself. He looked down the list, smiled and ticked her name off. 'I'm Felix, the stage manager,' he said. Then he directed another look at Sorcha.

'This is my friend,' said Allie. 'She's kind of like my assistant?' Felix looked rather bemused by this, as though he wasn't used to bit part players bringing their mates along to rehearsals.

'I'm afraid it's cast only in the rehearsal space,' he said apologetically. 'David's very strict about that. No exceptions.'

'Ah, don't sweat it,' said Sorcha. 'I know when I'm not wanted.' She indicated an open doorway that led down some steps into what looked like a bar area. 'I'll wait in there,' she said. 'If you need anything, just give me a shout.'

'The bar's not actually open at the moment,' said Felix, trying to be helpful, but Sorcha ignored him and wandered down the steps into the adjoining room. Felix smiled helplessly and shrugged his shoulders. He turned back to Allie. 'You're the first one here,' he told her.

'I'm early for everything,' she assured him.

'Well, that's a novelty,' he muttered. 'I wish there were more like you. It's your first time with us, isn't it?'

Allie nodded.

'In that case, I think I'd better take you across the road to the rehearsal space and you can say hello to David?'

'Oh, we don't rehearse here then?' asked Allie, trying not to sound disappointed.

'No, we won't be on the actual stage for a few weeks yet. Follow me.'

171

He led her back out through the main entrance and across the cobbled street to a shabby-looking doorway. He punched in a four digit code, pushed the door open and led Allie into a dingy hallway and up a steep flight of stone steps. They emerged into a huge room, the wooden floor of which had been divided up with long strips of different coloured tape. David was seated at a trestle table on the far side of the room, studying some papers. Empty chairs lined both sides of the table, each seat with a script in front of it. He looked up as Allie and Felix entered.

'Ah,' he said. 'Somebody's punctual. Allie, isn't it?' He stood up and shook her hand. He was a young, slim, bearded man with unkempt brown hair and soulful brown eyes. 'Great to have you on board,' he said and managed to actually sound like he meant it. He indicated a coffee machine standing on a small table in the corner of the room, together with cups, milk and biscuits. 'Why don't you help yourself to some refreshments while we wait for the others,' he suggested. He pointed to a large cardboard model standing on a table at the other end of the room. 'And you can be the first to check out our set.'

'Our set?' echoed Allie, mystified.

'Yes,' said David, smiling. 'We're really excited about it. Miroslav has based his design on a slaughterhouse.'

'Cool,' said Allie and hoped that was the right response.

'I'll head back and wrangle the others up,' announced Felix and he left.

Allie went over to the refreshments table and got herself a cup of coffee. David followed her over.

'I've been hearing some very good things about you,' he told her.

'Oh, really?' she murmured warily.

'Yes. I spoke to Martin Pringle, the other day. He said

you were truly impressive in his play at The Traverse. I wish I'd had a chance to see it.'

She shrugged. 'Oh, you didn't miss much,' she assured him.

'That's not what Martin said,' he told her. 'He told me that they had to extend the run to accommodate the demand for tickets. That's not something that happens too often.' He grinned. 'I hope you don't think it's too much of a step down, going back to a smaller role.'

'Not at all,' she said. 'Besides, my manager thinks it will be really good experience for me.'

'Oh yes, I had a quick chat with him after the audition. Interesting guy. All that stuff about Sean Connery. Amazing.'

Allie raised her eyebrows. 'Sean Connery?' she muttered.

'Yes, about giving him his first start in the business. Incredible. I have to say he's in great shape for someone his age.'

'Sean Connery?'

'No, your manager!'

Allie filled a mug with coffee. 'How old would you say he is?' she ventured.

'Well, he looks around fifty, I suppose, but he must be way older than that, mustn't he? I mean, Connery, that would be the early nineteen-sixties, right?' He waited for an answer but when he didn't get one, he continued. 'I must say, I'm impressed that you already have a manager so early in your career, especially such an influential one. How did you swing that?'

Allie shrugged. 'He… spotted me, I suppose. He has an eye for new talent.' She added milk to her mug. 'Anyway, he thinks this is the right move for me. And I'm just so excited to have the chance of working with Roxanne Walsh. She's sort of my acting hero.'

David grinned, nodded. 'That's nice,' he said. 'You'd be surprised how many people have said that to me. I've known her for years, of course. We first worked together at the Contact Theatre in Manchester. Real seat of the pants stuff, you know? No scripts, total improv. But Roxanne was in her element. Oh, she's a force of nature, that one!' Allie smiled and nodded, but she didn't really have the first idea what he was on about.

Pretty soon, the other actors started to arrive, wandering into the room one after the other and, every time somebody came through the door, David took the trouble to introduce them to Allie. It wasn't just actors. There was a lighting designer and a musical director and some people with job descriptions she really couldn't begin to fathom the meaning of. A tall bearded man strode into the room, looking pretty self-important and David told Allie that this was Victor McInnery, who would be playing the role of John Proctor. Victor took Allie's hand in his, almost crushing it in his enthusiasm and gave her a devil-may-care grin.

'A real pleasure,' he purred, in a deep Glaswegian accent. 'You're fresh out of drama school, no doubt?'

'Er... no,' said Allie, surprised. 'Should I be?'

'Not at all! I just assumed with you being so young and all...'

'No,' said Allie and there was an uncomfortable silence. 'I... I never actually went to drama school,' she added.

Just then, another man came into the room and Victor turned away without a word and hurried over to greet him, which Allie felt was pretty rude. All right, so she only had a small role in this production, but that didn't mean she was a nobody.

It was a large cast and most of them seemed to already know each other. Their various names passed mostly over Allie's head, but she did take note when a tall, stately-looking woman arrived and David introduced her to Allie as Olivia Quinn, who he said would be playing the role of Goody Proctor.

'Olivia, of course, has just had a huge hit on the telly,' added David. 'I'm sure you've seen the detective series, Grangemouth?'

'Of course,' said Allie. She'd never heard of it but wasn't going to admit that. She made a mental note to try and find out more about it. Olivia seemed to study Allie intently as she shook her hand, her slightly downturned mouth suggesting that she didn't much like what she was looking at.

'My God,' she said, 'you know you're getting old when actors start looking like they're barely out of school!'

Allie felt embarrassed by the remark and shocked that anyone would speak their mind so openly. 'I'm older than I look!' she protested.

Olivia's expression suggested she wasn't really interested either way.

'Allie's just had a hit at The Traverse,' said David, clearly trying to change the subject, but Olivia's impassive face didn't change one jot. She didn't actually say, 'So what?' but it was right there in her demeanour and Allie made a mental note to be careful what she said to Ms. Quinn, who was evidently a bit of a madam.

Soon, everyone was present except for Roxanne Walsh. David suggested that they all take a seat around the long table and do some basic introductions. Allie found herself sitting alongside the three young actors who would be playing Abigail's other girls. They were Kim and Sarah and Louise and they all seemed highly excited to be there. It turned out they were indeed fresh out of their respective drama schools and, like Allie, thrilled to be working alongside the famous Roxanne Walsh. They asked where Allie was from and when she simply told them 'The Quartermile', they looked suitably envious. Kim said that she was in a tiny bedsit on Fountainbridge, while the other two were still living with their parents. 'I'd love to have my own place,' said Sarah wistfully.

The introductions began. Allie made a pretence of listening to them, but her gaze kept straying to the door, anticipating the imminent arrival of her idol. When it came to her turn, she just mumbled something about her recent appearance at The Traverse and how she was hoping to develop her career.

Next, David did a little talk about his love for *The Crucible*, his ambitions for this production and the main things he hoped to achieve with it. He'd been talking for perhaps ten minutes or so when the door crashed open and Roxanne Walsh finally bustled in.

Allie felt a strange thrill go through her. The face that was looking apologetically around the room was one she knew so well from television, film and theatre, and though she looked somehow slightly different in real life, still it was unmistakably her: the same ageless elfin face, the same short cropped blonde hair, the same keen blue eyes. She was dressed as though she'd thrown on whatever came to hand that morning – a pair of black leggings, a faded Amnesty International T-shirt and an oversized denim jacket, yet she looked somehow like she'd just stepped off the pages of a fashion magazine. And when she spoke, there was that unmistakable Mancunian accent, effortlessly working-class but at the same time, absolutely classless. 'Sorry, guys, didn't realise how long it would take me to walk up here from Stockbridge.'

'There are such things as taxis,' murmured Olivia, as though Roxanne's lateness had caused untold problems.

'Can't do that, chuck.' Roxanne waved her arm and showed everyone at the table the Fitbit around her wrist, currently showing a figure of twelve thousand and twenty one. 'Got to keep me step count up, haven't I?' She grinned. 'How are you, Olivia? Keeping well?'

'Oh, tolerable, I suppose,' said Olivia, in a tone that suggested she was actually at death's door.

'Caught you in that new detective series,' added Roxanne. 'Bloody brilliant.'

'Oh, did you really think so?' Olivia's stern countenance rearranged itself into a smile, which Allie told herself was probably a rare event.

'Are you kidding? It was genius. I fully expect to hear your name mentioned at the next BAFTAs.' Now Roxanne turned her attention to David. 'Sorry, Davie, I've had a bit of a time of it this morning. Have I missed much?'

'No worries,' he assured her. 'Come and meet everyone. We'll start over.'

Nobody seemed to object to this, so Roxanne went around the long table, making a point of shaking hands with everyone and exchanging a few words. When she came to Victor, she said something about a production of *Waiting For Godot* she'd seen at the Edinburgh Festival years ago and how his performance as Vladimir had stayed with her long afterwards. Victor was clearly delighted at this news, virtually purring like a big, contented cat. Allie noticed the way he checked out the reactions of the others around the table, to gauge how impressed they were by this brief exchange. Allie waited nervously, trying to think of something she might say to her idol that wouldn't sound totally idiotic but when she heard the simpering platitudes that Kim, Sarah and Louise came out with, she thought she'd do better to rein it back a few notches. She was actually the last person at the table to speak and ended up simply saying, 'Hi, Roxanne, I'm Allie Lawrence. I'm a big fan.'

'Allie Lawrence?' echoed Roxanne, as though the name was familiar to her. 'Allie Lawrence. Now where have I... hey, you're not the girl I read about in *The Guardian*? The one who did the show at The Traverse?'

Allie was suddenly aware that every eye at the table had turned in her direction and she felt her face reddening under such intense scrutiny. 'Er, yeah,' she whispered. 'That was me, actually.'

'Wow. That was a review to die for,' said Roxanne, grinning. 'God, I wish I'd had a chance to see that show. Sounds right up my street. And am I correct, that it was your first time out?'

'Yes. Yes, that's right.'

'Hey, go you.' Roxanne mimed a punch to Allie's shoulder and she nearly died of pleasure. Roxanne indicated a vacant chair next to Allie. 'Anybody sitting there?' she asked.

'Er, no,' murmured Allie.

'Great.' Roxanne stepped around the end of the table and slipped into it. 'You don't mind if I park me carcass here, do ya?'

'Umm... no... please, I...'

'Perhaps you'd be happier up here with Victor and Olivia,' suggested David. 'So you leads can–'

'No, I'm good here,' insisted Roxanne. She gave Allie a sly wink. 'Maybe if I sit next to you, some of your magic will rub off on me,' she whispered. 'I'd kill for a review like that.'

Allie almost gasped out loud at this. Right now, she felt like her seat was ascending into the sky like a rocket ship. She was aware of the envious looks she was getting from the three drama school girls and she honestly couldn't remember when she had last felt this happy. Roxanne Walsh had remembered her name! She had chosen to sit right beside her!

The read-through progressed at a leisurely pace through the day and Allie kept her attention firmly on Roxanne, noting the way she read her lines with absolute authority, the way that even sitting here in this little room, she seemed to totally inhabit the role of Abigail Williams, making herself seem somehow much younger than her actual age. *I could learn something here*, Allie told herself. She thought about the way Roxanne, a huge star, had greeted her, making Allie feel like she was the important one. Roxanne had pulled the same trick on Victor and Olivia. And it all made absolute sense. Most of the actors in this room had worked together before and had already established friendships. Roxanne was the blow-in, the one who had been brought in to give the production star power and it would have been so easy for the others to resent her – but she had effortlessly charmed her way into their good books, simply by diverting all the attention to them. It occurred to Allie that Nick worked in very much the same way, though with Roxanne the process felt much kinder, more authentic.

They broke for lunch at one o' clock and the cast headed off in all directions to pick up their food. Allie remembered Sorcha, so on the pretext of going to use the toilet, she found her way back to the street and went across the road to the theatre. She found her friend still slumped at an empty table in the bar, looking really bored. 'Hey,' she said, brightening when Allie appeared. 'How's it going over there?'

'It's going great,' said Allie. 'Have you been sitting here all this time?'

'Sure. I said I'd be here if you needed me, didn't I?'

Allie frowned. 'But that's crazy. We're going to be working here till late afternoon. You should go and do something.'

Sorcha looked at her blankly. 'Such as?' she said.

'I don't know. Go down the shops or find a bar or something. Honestly, it's daft sitting here bored out of your mind, isn't it?'

Sorcha seemed doubtful. 'Nick wouldn't be pleased if he found out,' she said. 'I'm supposed to stick with you at all times. That's how it works. And anyway, I've got nothing else to do.'

'That's crazy. Don't you have any interests?'

Sorcha shrugged. 'I'm here to wait on you,' she said. 'That's my assignment. There isn't anything else.'

'But aren't you bored?'

'Sweetie, you've no idea,' Sorcha assured her. 'The first hundred years or so, that was boring. I've gone way beyond that.'

Just then, Roxanne came down the steps into the bar, talking animatedly on her mobile phone and clearly unaware that there was anybody else in the room.

'But that's ridiculous,' she said. 'There must be somebody who can fix it.' She went and sat at a table a short distance away, her back turned to Allie and Sorcha. 'I'm afraid it isn't,' she said. 'There's no hot water at all. Well, maybe it was working perfectly yesterday but I can assure you... look, I'm going to be here for the best part of a month and if you think I'm showering in freezing cold water every day, I... Well, I can't help it if the owners are away, you just need to...' She broke off and looked at her phone in dismay. 'And good day to you!' she snapped. She glanced up, finally noticed Allie and Sorcha and appeared to be genuinely mortified. 'Oh, I'm sorry, I didn't see you sitting there!' she said. She waved her phone. 'Either we got cut off or he just hung up on me.'

'Problem?' asked Allie, mystified.

'Oh, it's just this apartment I've rented. It looked great on the internet, you know, but all kinds of things aren't working at the moment. I arrived late last night, all ready for bed and there was a student party going on until four a.m. I mean, I like a party as much as the next person, but four a.m.? I didn't get to sleep until six. Then I jumped in the shower this morning and it was bloody freezing! They must have heard the scream in Glasgow! And they're telling me they can't get anybody out to it until next week.'

Sorcha scowled. 'That sucks,' she said. 'You should tell 'em to stuff their apartment.'

Roxanne shook her head. 'Might not be the best move, chuck. Have you any idea how hard it is to find decent accommodation in this city?'

Sorcha looked slyly at Allie. 'Some of us don't seem to have any trouble,' she said. 'Do we, Allie?'

Allie shrugged. 'I suppose not,' she said, sheepishly.

'Yes, well, sorry to inflict all that on you. I only came in here cos I thought it was empty.' Roxanne got up to leave but in the same moment, Allie had what felt like a brilliant idea.

'Wait,' she said. 'Roxanne... Miss Walsh... why not stay with us?'

Roxanne hesitated. 'Come again?' she said.

'We've got loads of room, haven't we?' said Allie, looking at Sorcha.

Sorcha scowled. 'Oh, I don't know about–'

'We're just around the corner from here on the Quartermile, a lovely big flat. There's a spare bedroom and everything.'

Roxanne looked nonplussed. 'Oh no, I couldn't let you...'

'Yes you could! Why not?'

'Allie,' murmured Sorcha. 'I'm not sure Nick...'

'It's really lovely there, I know you'd like it. And it would be great to have some company, wouldn't it, Sorcha?'

Sorcha's expression seemed to say otherwise but from where she was standing, Roxanne couldn't see that.

'Oh, I get it.' Roxanne seemed to be considering the idea. 'You mean, if I pay you the rent instead of these other people. Only I'm not sure I can get out of the contract at such short notice.'

'It doesn't matter about the money,' Allie assured her, with a wave of her hand. 'The thing is, we've got plenty of room and we'd love to have you. Why not come and have a wee look after we've finished here and see what you think?'

Roxanne seemed to be pondering the matter. 'Look, it's really lovely of you to offer, but...'

Allie suddenly felt super-confident. 'No "buts",' she said. 'And don't decide until you've actually seen the place. Really, we're fifteen minutes walk from here, right beside the Meadows. You'll love it.'

Roxanne smiled and her whole face seemed to light up. 'Ah, thanks chuck, that's really kind of you.' She shrugged her shoulders. 'Yeah, OK, I'll come and have a look later on. But I'm not staying there for free, we'll have to work out some kind of rent.' She slipped her phone back into her pocket. 'Well, I'm going to go and grab a butty from somewhere and head back to the Green Room.'

'Yeah, see you there in a bit,' said Allie.

Roxanne turned and went up the stairs into the foyer and Sorcha looked at Allie accusingly. 'I don't know what Nick will have to say about this,' she warned. 'Sub-letting the apartment.'

'Nick won't know,' said Allie, dismissively.

'Oh, you think?' Sorcha sneered. 'Of course he'll know. You can't let out a sly fart without him knowing.'

Allie shrugged. 'Well, he can't complain,' she said. 'I'm only doing stuff to further my career. That's what he wants, isn't it?'

Sorcha scowled and nodded towards the stairs. 'Who is she, anyway? Her face is kind of familiar.'

'Are you kidding? That's Roxanne Walsh.'

'Oh wait. Is she the one used to be in *The Canteen*?'

'Well, yes, a long time ago,' said Allie. 'That was her first TV show.'

'It's always on Dave though,' said Sorcha. 'Crikey, she's lost a lot of weight, hasn't she?'

'Yeah, careful what you say about that. Body shaming isn't cool. And she's only like my biggest hero in the entire world.'

'Clearly not as big a hero as she used to be.'

'I mean it, Sorcha! No more nasty comments. If I could be a tenth as good an actor as her, I'd be happy.' She sighed. 'I'd better get back to it,' she announced. 'I need to get something to eat.'

'Hold on a minute.' Sorcha leaned forward to root in her

handbag and pulled out a Tupperware box. She handed it to Allie.

'What's this?' she asked.

'What do you think it is? It's your packed lunch. Smoked salmon and cream cheese bagel with a green salad and a strawberry yoghurt. Oh, yeah, and a diet coke. I thought of everything.'

'But when did you…?'

'This morning before I brought in your breakfast.'

Allie shook her head. 'You really look after me, don't you?' she murmured.

'I aim to please. Now, what do you want me to do in the meantime?'

Allie thought about it for a moment. 'Maybe–'

'Yeah?'

'Maybe head back to the flat and clean out the spare bedroom?' she said. 'Just in case Roxanne decides to move in.'

'The spare bedroom.' Sorcha fixed her with a stare. 'You mean my room.'

Allie flinched. She hadn't really thought about it like that. 'Oh, sorry, Sorcha,' she said. 'I wasn't thinking. But, well, it's not as if you–'

'As if I what?'

'It's not as if you ever go in there, is it? It's not like you ever sleep. And don't pretend that you do, because I know better. I've never known you go to sleep. You're there on the sofa watching the telly when I go to bed and you're there with the breakfast when I wake up. Sometimes I wake in the middle of the night and I can hear the TV. So you obviously sit on the sofa watching the goggle box all night long.'

'Yeah,' muttered Sorcha. 'Well, that's what you do when you're dead.'

Allie winced. 'Please don't say that,' she whispered.

Sorcha shrugged. 'You're the boss,' she said.

'No, I'm not the boss. Not really. I'd like to think that we're friends.'

'Friends, eh?' Sorcha smiled bleakly. 'Well, there's a novel twist.' She shrugged, sighed. 'OK, I'll go and clean up for Lady Muck. Perhaps you'd like me to put out a red carpet while I'm there?'

'Think you could get hold of one?' asked Allie, smiling sweetly to show she was only joking. 'All right, I'll catch up with you later.'

And with that, she went up the stairs to the foyer and made her way back over to the rehearsal room.

20

THE GUEST

Roxanne looked slowly around the interior of the lounge, which had been freshly tidied, dusted and hoovered to within an inch of its life by Sorcha. She was standing in one corner of the room, arms crossed, a defiant expression on her face, as though daring Roxanne to say anything critical. But it was evident that she was very impressed,

'Allie, this place is fantastic,' she said. 'This is a rental?'

Allie nodded. 'That's right,' she said.

'Must be costing you a bomb. How do you…?' She broke off as though sensing that she might be about to say too much.

'Afford it?' Allie prompted her, amused by Roxanne's discomfort.

'Oh no, I didn't mean–'

'Sure you did. But don't worry. I totally get it. I mean, how does somebody who's just starting out afford all this, right?'

'Look, I really didn't.'

'The fact is, my manager takes care of it all.'

Roxanne's blue eyes widened in disbelief, then narrowed suspiciously. 'Really?' she murmured. 'How does that work?'

'It's complicated,' admitted Allie. She gestured to the sofa. 'Make yourself comfortable,' she suggested. 'Coffee?'

'I'd love one,' said Roxanne settling herself onto the plush leather. 'If it's not too much trouble.'

'None at all.' Allie sat beside her, then turned to look at Sorcha. 'Two coffees,' she said, then remembered to add, 'Please.' Sorcha rolled her eyes but turned obediently on her heel and marched out of the room.

Roxanne gazed after her. 'What's the story with her?' she asked.

'Oh, Sorcha's just a pal.' Allie registered Roxanne's quizzical expression and added, 'Well, more of a PA, really.'

'And does she always wait on you like that?

'She does when she's in the right mood.'

'I see. Must be nice to have somebody to take care of that kind of stuff.' She shook her head. 'OK, so tell me more about this manager of yours. You say he's paying the rent on this place?'

'Sure. Don't you have a manager?'

Roxanne grimaced. 'I have an agent,' she said. 'He takes fifteen percent of everything I earn. He certainly doesn't pay out for stuff. If I asked him to fund something like this he'd have a hissy fit.' Now she looked concerned. 'Allie, you sure this guy is trustworthy?'

'Oh, well, I wouldn't say that exactly. But he knows how to get me things. People find it very hard to say no to him.' She made an effort to change the subject. 'How are you liking being Abigail?'

Roxanne chuckled. 'That's an odd way of putting it!' she said. 'As though you actually become the person you're playing.'

'Well, don't you?'

'Only while you're on stage, love. The trick is being able to switch off afterwards and go back to being yourself.'

She considered for a moment. 'I'm loving it, though. Always wanted to play Abigail, but never got the chance till now. When I heard David was planning a production, I got in there sharpish! Kept pestering him to let me have a go, even though we both know I'm too old for it.'

'Not at all,' said Allie.

'You're very kind, but I'm afraid so,' Roxanne assured her. 'And it's like David said, there's nothing in the text that says Abigail has to be a kid. "We can play her as a more mature character," he said. "Sure we can!" I think he was trying to convince himself more than anything. And it's all a bit bonkers because Abigail isn't even supposed to be the lead, but David decided to pitch it that way.'

'It's your name on the programme,' Allie reminded her. 'And your face on the posters. So it kind of is the lead role.'

'Yeah, I know.' Roxanne grimaced and shook her head. 'What can you do? David reckons we can swing it, so, I keep asking myself, what's the worst that can happen? The critics will make a few snide comments about me being mutton dressed as lamb. I've had worse.' She studied Allie for a moment. 'Really, Abigail should be played by someone your age.'

'I have studied the part,' said Allie.

'Have you now?' Roxanne looked genuinely interested. 'Where was that?'

Allie thought about trotting out the lie that Sorcha had come up with, but decided instead to tell the truth. 'At school,' she said. 'For my drama exam. It's what made me decide I wanted to be an actor in the first place. I even did some of it for my audition for this show. Bit cheeky, I know, but I knew Abigail so well. She's kind of like my role model.' She snapped quickly into character and quoted a few lines. 'We did dance, Uncle, and when you leaped out of the bushes so suddenly, Betty was frightened and then she fainted. And there's the whole of it.' She gave a little bow and Roxanne applauded.

'Very impressive,' she said.

Allie studied her hands, feeling suddenly awkward. 'Not a patch on you, of course,' she murmured.

'Don't be daft, I bet you were great. And it got you the part you were after, didn't it? Not the same as doing a lead role, I know, but it's early days yet. Golly, when I think of some of the crap I did when I was just out of drama school–' She frowned. 'Which one did you go to, by the way?' she asked.

'I didn't,' said Allie. 'But Miss Marchmont reckoned I was a natural.'

'Who's Miss Marchmont when she's at home?'

'My drama teacher. At school.'

'Well, I do get it. I had a teacher who encouraged me, back in the day. I wouldn't be where I am now without her getting me started. And you clearly know the role really well.' Roxanne seemed to think about that for a moment. 'Hey, you know what? You should understudy me.'

Allie looked up at her alarmed. 'Oh, I don't think so!' she protested.

'Yeah, seriously, why not? We haven't fixed one up yet. I bet you could do a great job of it, if push came to shove?'

'Well, I suppose, but–'

'It makes perfect sense. I'll have a word with David.' She leaned closer. 'Don't go getting your hopes up though,' she whispered. 'I'm never ill!'

'As if I'd be good enough to take your place,' said Allie.

'Don't be so modest. I saw that review. Mark Rillington, wasn't it? Jesus. He seemed to think you were the next big thing.'

'Yeah, well, I guess he was in a generous mood that day.'

'So modest!' Roxanne chuckled. 'So where are you from, Allie?'

'Oh, a wee village in Perthshire. You wouldn't have heard of it.'

'I might have. Try me.'

'It's called Killiecrankie.'

They looked at each other for a moment, then Roxanne laughed. 'No, fair play, that's a new one on me!'

'It's not much of a place, but it's where I grew up.'

'I'm sure it's lovely. I've been all over the place, me. I did a Summer Season in Morecambe, me first year out of drama school. Died on me arse every night for three weeks. That was fun.' She rolled her eyes, then studied Allie for a while, seemingly amused by her. 'I'm not being funny, chuck, but, you don't really seem old enough to be this far along with your career. How long ago did you actually finish school?'

'I didn't exactly finish. I left. About a month ago.'

'What, just like that? Are you allowed to do that?'

'Looks like it. Nobody's come after me, anyway,' said Allie. 'I came to Edinburgh a few weeks ago. The Traverse show was my first time out.'

Roxanne actually gasped at that. 'What, you're saying you went straight from school into a speaking role? In a matter of days? How did you swing that?'

Allie nodded. 'Nick got it for me.'

'Your manager? Hecky thump, he must be good!'

Allie grimaced. 'That wouldn't be the word I'd use to describe him,' she said. 'But he usually gets his own way.'

Just then, Sorcha clumped into the room carrying a tray containing coffee mugs, a cafetiere and a plate of posh biscuits. She brought them over and set them down on a low table.

'Want me to serve?' she asked Allie.

'No, that's all right, we'll sort ourselves out.' Allie glanced at Roxanne. 'You're welcome to stay for dinner if you like,' she said. 'We're having...' She looked at Sorcha. 'What are you cooking?' she asked.

'Whatever you fancy, Sweetie.' She looked at Roxanne. 'Maybe we should let our esteemed guest choose,' she said, making no attempt to hide the sarcasm in her voice. 'I'm sure she's no stranger to a slap-up meal.' She ignored the fierce glare that Allie directed at her.

'Er, no, that's all right,' Roxanne assured her. 'I said I'd eat with David and his wife tonight. Thanks, anyway.'

'Pity,' said Sorcha. 'You could do with feeding up. Get you back to the way you used to be.'

Roxanne stared at her. 'I beg your pardon,' she said.

'You'd better get back to the kitchen,' said Allie, briskly, and watched as Sorcha strode out of the room. She picked up the cafetiere and filled a couple of mugs. 'Help yourself to milk and sugar,' she added.

'What did she mean by that?' asked Roxanne. 'The way I used to be? Here, was she having a dig at...?'

'Oh no, don't take it the wrong way! She's just a big fan of *The Canteen*.'

Roxanne raised her eyebrows. 'Blimey,' she said. 'Do people still watch that?' She shook her head. 'It was my first real TV show. Well, apart from a walk-on part in an episode of *Miss Marple*.' She shook her head. '2005,' she murmured. 'Seems like a hundred years ago.' She chuckled. 'And your friend preferred me doing that kind of stuff, did she?'

'Oh, I wouldn't worry about it. Sorcha is kind of weird,

you know. Spends all her time watching the telly. I really love what you're doing now.' She remembered something. 'Hey, I read that you played Macbeth in Manchester! I would have loved to have seen that.'

They fixed their coffees and sipped in silence for a little while. Roxanne kept casting appreciative looks out through the French window at the sunlit Meadows ahead of them.

'That'd be perfect for my morning run,' she said.

'Oh, you run do you?'

'Bit of an obsession these days,' said Roxanne. 'Well, you have to keep yourself strong and fit for this marlarky.' She laughed ruefully. 'You should try it. Running, I mean. Once you get the feel for it, it's the best.'

'Maybe I will,' said Allie. 'If you wouldn't mind a bit of company.'

'You'd be more than welcome.' Roxanne looked thoughtful. 'You're sure this is OK?' she asked eventually. 'Me staying here? It feels a little too good to be true, if you want me to be honest.'

'How d'you mean?'

'Well, it's just that in my experience, when people offer you something nice, they generally expect something in return. Like your manager, for instance. I mean, there isn't any... funny stuff going on, is there?'

'Oh no, nothing like that! I have to admit I had my doubts when I first met him, and he is kind of fanciable, if I'm honest, but no, he's not interested in that sort of thing.'

'He must be a very unusual bloke then. I generally find that's what most of them are interested in. Oh, some of them will deny it until they're blue in the face, but in the end they show their true colours.' She looked uncomfortable. 'But what I'm saying is, I hope you understand, chuck, I can't give you any help with your career. I don't have that kind of influence.' She gestured around the room. 'Not that it looks like you need any help,' she added. 'I can't afford a place like this now and I've been around the block a few times.'

'Oh, I wasn't asking, honestly. I just genuinely wanted to help you out.'

The doorbell rang, the noise shrilling through the apartment. 'I'll get it!' shouted Sorcha from the kitchen.

'I wonder who that is,' murmured Allie. But she knew exactly who it would be. After all, who else would be calling here? A minute later, Nick was strolling into the room. 'Allie, I hope you don't mind me dropping by, but I wanted to...' He broke off and did an exaggerated double take when he saw Roxanne. 'I'm so sorry,' he said, 'I had no idea you had company.'

Yeah, right, thought Allie.

His gaze focused and he gave a little gasp. He pointed at Roxanne. 'Oh my goodness,' he said. 'It's you, isn't it? It really is you!'

Roxanne seemed amused. 'Last time I checked,' she said.

'Oh, forgive me, I don't mean to stare, but I am such a fan of your work.'

Allie nearly laughed out loud at that, remembering that Nick hadn't even known who Roxanne was the first time that Allie had mentioned her name.

'Er, perhaps I should leave,' suggested Roxanne. 'If you two need to talk business, I don't want to–'

'Nonsense!' said Nick. 'I wouldn't hear of it.' He dropped into an armchair. 'I'm the one who called without checking it was OK to do so. Please, just pretend I'm not here.'

Just at that moment, Sorcha appeared carrying another

coffee mug. She went to the table, filled it from the cafetiere and handed it to Nick. Then without a word, she left the room.

'You two have got her well trained,' observed Roxanne, quietly, and Allie immediately felt a stab of guilt. Was that what she was doing? Taking Sorcha for granted? When she thought about it, she supposed that she was, but she really hadn't meant to do that. She told herself she needed to watch out for that in future. Privilege could kind of creep up on you, make you selfish. And Sorcha was supposed to be a friend, not a servant.

'She's a treasure,' said Nick, completely missing the tone of criticism in Roxanne's voice. 'Sorry, I haven't even introduced myself. I'm…'

'You're Nick,' said Roxanne, with an ironic smile; and when he looked surprised, she added, 'An educated guess. Allie was just telling me about you.'

'Nothing bad, I hope.' Nick leaned forward and extended a hand towards Roxanne. A business card seemed to sprout like magic from between his fingers. Roxanne took the card gingerly and studied it. 'If I can ever be of service,' murmured Nick, 'don't hesitate to call.'

'Nick Mahoun,' murmured Roxanne. She turned the card over, looking puzzled. 'But there's no phone number on here,' she said, waving the card. 'Or even an email. It's just your name.'

Nick smiled. 'Call anyway,' he said. 'I'll hear you.'

There was an uncomfortable silence. Roxanne slipped the card into her pocket and took another sip of coffee.

'I've invited Roxanne to stay with me,' said Allie, almost defiantly. 'The shower in her flat doesn't work. I thought she could have the spare room.'

'Capital suggestion,' said Nick. 'There's plenty of space

here.' He looked at Roxanne. 'If anything isn't to your liking, Miss Walsh, just mention it to Allie and I'll make sure it's sorted for you.'

'That's very kind of you, Mr Mahoun, but–'

'Nick. Just call me Nick. And, should you ever find yourself in need of management...'

'Oh, I think I'm managing quite well on me own, thanks.' Roxanne seemed both intrigued by Nick and wary of him. She studied him for a moment. 'Allie was telling me that you take care of the rent on this place.' Roxanne gestured around. 'That's quite an investment.'

Nick shrugged. 'True. But I'm a firm believer in the fact that talent will out eventually. When Allie is a star, then I shall think about recouping my costs.'

'You obviously have a lot of faith in her,' said Roxanne.

'Some people in this world are just naturals,' said Nick. 'Take yourself for instance, Miss Walsh. I'm sure there was somebody who spotted your abilities when you were starting out.'

'Not really,' said Roxanne. 'A teacher encouraged me at school. I was at a couple of youth theatres in me teens. I studied at a technical college and I eventually managed to get enough sponsorship to go to RADA.'

'Oh, that's nice,' said Nick, his expression blank.

'It was better than "nice",' Roxanne assured him. 'It opened doors for me. But it wasn't easy. I had to graft for it. Nobody handed me anything on a plate.'

'That's a pity.'

'Oh, but I don't think that it is.'

Nick smiled frostily. 'Really?'

'Yes, really. I've had to work bloody hard for everything I've achieved in this industry and in the long run, I think that makes me appreciate it a whole lot more. There are no easy rides in this business, Mr Mahoun, and in the end, everything has to be paid for.'

They sat there staring at each other for a moment and Allie was aware of waves of hostility generating from Roxanne. Eventually, Nick seemed to get the message. He shrugged his shoulders and got up from his chair.

'Still, for all that, circumstances can change. If you should ever find you have need of my services–'

'I think that's extremely unlikely,' said Roxanne.

'Then I'll bid you good day.' Nick turned slightly to look at Allie. 'Ah. The reason I dropped by,' he said. 'I was singing your praises earlier. To a gentleman by the name of Steve Seinfeld.'

Allie stared at him. 'The film director?' she murmured.

'Yes, that's the fellow. He's right here in Edinburgh as it happens. Apparently he's looking for a teenage girl to star in his new motion picture. I told him I might have the very person he's been searching for. Watch this space.' He turned and strolled away towards the door. 'I'll let myself out,' he called back to them.

In the silence that followed, Allie was aware of her heart beating a little faster. She listened as the front door of the flat opened and closed. Then she remembered to breathe. 'So that was Nick,' she said.

Roxanne's expression was unreadable. 'Do you mind if I tell you something?' she asked Allie.

'No, please go ahead.'

Roxanne pointed in the direction of the door. 'I don't like him. Not one little bit.'

Allie wasn't really surprised to hear this. It was clear that Roxanne and Nick hadn't exactly hit it off.

'He's… unusual,' she ventured.

'That's not the word I'd use to describe him. "Creepy"

would sum him up better. I mean, how old is he exactly?'

'I'm not sure. How old does he look to you?'

'I dunno. Around my age, I suppose?'

'Right.'

'And he claims to be an expert at this stuff, OK? But when I mentioned RADA to him, his expression never changed. It was like he'd never heard of the place. He hadn't the foggiest idea that he was supposed to be impressed.'

'He can seem a bit out of touch sometimes,' admitted Allie. 'But you heard what he said. Steve Seinfeld–'

'Oh, you believed that, did you?' Roxanne shook her head. 'I hate to be the bearer of bad news, chuck, but that was a lie.'

'What makes you say that?'

'I took a call from my agent on the way over here. Quite by coincidence, he told me that one of his other clients, a good mate of mine, is currently working on Seinfeld's new movie.'

'I don't understand.'

'It's just started shooting. In New Zealand.'

'Oh.'

'So quite how Mr Seinfeld has managed to whiz over to Edinburgh for a quick chat with Mr Mahoun is beyond me.'

Allie shook her head. 'Well, all right,' she said. 'But Nick did get me the audition at The Traverse. And the one for our play.'

'He may have got you the auditions, chuck, but you got the parts. Don't forget that.' Roxanne sighed, shook her head. 'Look, maybe I'm talking out of turn, here, and maybe I'm talking my way out of staying in this lovely apartment, too, but you be bloody careful. If your so-called manager is openly lying to you, who knows where it might end?' She considered for a moment. 'You er... haven't signed anything with him, have you?'

Allie felt distinctly uncomfortable now. 'Well, I have, actually,' she said.

Roxanne looked worried at this news. 'Just do me a favour, will you? Be careful.' Roxanne set down her coffee mug and got up from her seat. 'Now look, if it's still OK with you, I'm going to head back to those dodgy lodgings of mine, and pick up me bags. But if you've changed your mind, I won't blame you one little bit. Speak now or forever keep your gob shut.'

Allie chuckled. 'No, really, it's all right.' She also got to her feet. 'I know you mean well. And I'd love you to come and stay, honestly I would.'

'Well, all right, then. Thanks.' Roxanne put her hands on Allie's shoulders and gave her an affectionate peck on the cheek. 'I'll be back in an hour or so,' she said. 'But I did promise to meet David for dinner later on, so–'

'That's cool. There's a spare set of keys somewhere, I'll look them out for you.' She walked Roxanne out of the lounge to the front door. 'Just buzz me when you get back and I'll let you in,' she said.

Roxanne smiled. 'Thanks again for this, Allie. You're a lifesaver.' She went out onto the landing and walked towards the lift.

Allie closed the door and went into the kitchen. She found Sorcha sitting at the breakfast bar, in front of a chopping board containing slices of onion and red pepper. A half-empty glass of white wine stood beside the board. Her face was expressionless but it was clear that she'd been listening in on the conversation.

'She needs to be careful,' said Sorcha. 'Questioning

Nick like that. He doesn't take kindly to that sort of thing.' She sliced an onion in half to emphasise the point she was making.

'Ah, she's all right,' said Allie. 'I really like her. I think she'll be a good friend to me.' She looked at Sorcha. 'You should lay off with the bitchy comments, though. All that stuff about the weight she's lost.'

Sorcha affected a look of hurt innocence. 'What bitchy comments?' she murmured. 'That was supposed to be a compliment.'

'It really didn't come out that way,' Allie assured her. She gestured to the chopping board. 'What are you making?' she asked.

'It doesn't have a name,' admitted Sorcha. 'If it's halfway edible, my work here is done.' She lifted her wine glass and waggled it invitingly. 'I don't suppose I can interest you in one of these.'

'I shouldn't,' said Allie.

But of course, she did.

21

RUNNING ON EMPTY

Allie pounded down the tarmac track that looped the Meadows, running alongside the lithe figure of Roxanne and just about managing to keep up with her. She glanced up to her left as they passed the Quartermile for the third time and there was Sorcha, standing on the balcony of the apartment, smoking a cigarette and looking impassively down at them.

On the first night that Roxanne had stayed at the apartment, she had announced her intention of going for a run the following morning before rehearsals and had invited Allie to join her. Though she had never really done any proper running in her life, Allie had accepted the offer and she wasn't at all surprised, later that night, when she looked in her bedroom wardrobe and found a selection of top-of-the-range jogging clothes arranged neatly on hangers, together with some state-of-the-art Nike running shoes. Naturally, when she tried on a Gore-Tex top and a pair of jogging pants, they fit her perfectly.

The first morning's efforts had half-killed her and Roxanne had been obliged to slow her own pace in order not to leave her companion far behind. But Allie had refused to give up and had gone out every morning since, getting a little better each time, though she was all too aware that if Roxanne had wanted to, she could easily have left her in her wake. But Roxanne wasn't competitive like that. She always ensured that she matched her pace to Allie's, so the two of them could chat as they went around. And they did chat, about pretty much everything: life, love, the whole shebang. Allie now knew that Roxanne was in a serious relationship with a guy called Adam, back in Manchester, a film editor at Media City – and that the two of them had been trying for kids for several years without success. They seemed devoted to each other though, and Roxanne phoned him on her mobile, every evening without fail, chatting away happily for up to an hour.

Allie had also discovered something entirely unexpected about this new routine: that she was enjoying her morning runs – indeed, she was absolutely loving them. It was a great way to clear her mind and get her properly awake; to make her aware of muscles in her legs that she hadn't even realised were there.

After they had finished running, she and Roxanne would head back to the flat for well-earned showers and emerge to find that Sorcha had their breakfast all ready to go. Then they would put on sweatshirts and leggings and walk side-by-side to the Lyceum to rehearse. As they walked, Allie noticed the sly looks that passers-by gave Roxanne, clearly recognising her. Those who were bold enough to speak to her always got a cheery greeting and even an autograph if they asked for one. Sorcha, of course, always insisted on accompanying them to the theatre, following at a discreet distance, keeping a careful eye on them. Allie was aware that Roxanne was beginning to feel uncomfortable about this. 'It's a wonder she doesn't insist on running with us every morning,' she muttered one time, and Allie had giggled at the idea, trying to imagine Sorcha in her heavy Doc Marten's, thudding grimly along the track behind them.

'She's just looking out for me,' said Allie protectively.

'She's like a flipping shadow,' muttered Roxanne. 'I'm amazed she doesn't follow you into the toilet. And anyway, aren't you a little old to be needing a chaperone?'

As the days slipped steadily by, rehearsals had become more serious and much more complicated – there were costumes to try on, make up tests to experiment with. There were press calls for photography and, for Roxanne especially, lengthy interviews with the press. There was no doubting that she had the lead role in this production. It was always her name singled out from the other performers for a special mention. Now, three weeks after the process had begun, they had been through dress rehearsals and the final tech rehearsal and were only hours away from the very first performance of *The Crucible*.

Allie and Roxanne reached the agreed finishing point for their third circuit and slowed to a walk, both of them panting and sweating profusely. Around them the daily traffic of the Meadows ebbed and flowed. Mothers pushed buggies, en route for coffee with friends. Students with rucksacks headed off for their first lessons of the day. Cyclists sped by in tight fitting Lycra and elaborate multi-coloured helmets that made them look like huge exotic insects, while on the running track beside them, joggers thudded gamely alongside, headphones in their ears, lost in their own personal soundtracks. Allie reflected that she was living in one of the most vibrant cities on the planet and tonight she would be appearing in a major theatrical production alongside one of the best-known actors in the UK. It felt unreal, like some kind of elaborate dream she was having.

Only it wasn't a dream, she reminded herself. This was reality.

'You OK?' Roxanne asked, linking an arm through Allie's.

Allie nodded. 'I'm fine,' she gasped. She was still trying to get her breath back to its regular rhythm.

'Not too nervous about tonight?'

'Nah. It's easy for me. I don't have that much to do. What about you?'

'Oh, I'm always nervous. Especially when we don't have the safety net of a couple of preview nights. Not as bad as I used to be, mind. In the early days I used to throw up before I went on stage. Happened every time.'

'No way,' said Allie.

'Seriously, I'm not exaggerating. I've got it under control now, but I still get the collywobbles.'

'Have you decided what you're doing next?'

Roxanne had confided in Allie that she was currently weighing up two TV offers she'd had – one for a drama set in medieval England and another, a true crime story from the 1960s, in which she would portray a notorious female murderer. 'I'm gravitating towards the psychopath,' she said with a cheerful grin. 'I reckon it would be the bigger challenge.'

'You like a challenge, don't you?' said Allie.

'Yeah, I suppose so. I reckon most people do, don't they?'

Allie shrugged. 'I wouldn't say that,' she muttered. 'A lot of people prefer an easy life. My parents, for instance.'

Roxanne looked interested. 'I think that's the first time I've ever heard you mention them,' she observed. 'What's the story, morning glory? Don't you get on with 'em?'

'Oh, they're OK, I suppose.'

'Are they still back in… what's it called? Killiecrankie?'

Allie nodded. 'They love it there. They'll never leave.'

Roxanne seemed amused by Allie's despondent expression. 'And what did they think of you running off to the big city at the tender age of sixteen?'

'They weren't best pleased. In fact, they were going to set the polis on me. But Nick talked them round.'

Roxanne shook her head. 'Nick again. Is there anyone that man can't charm the pants off?'

'Well, you for a start,' said Allie and they both laughed at that.

'I dunno exactly what it is about him,' said Roxanne. 'But he gives me the shivers.' She glanced at Allie. 'No offence, love.'

'None taken. And I do get it.'

They walked back around to the entrance of the Quartermile. It was another fine, sunny day with a refreshing breeze that cooled the sweat on Allie's forehead. Up in the apartment, they each had a quick shower and then headed to the kitchen where Sorcha had their breakfast ready for them: scrambled eggs, wholemeal toast and coffee.

'I'm going to miss this when I head back to Manchester,' sighed Roxanne, as she and Allie settled themselves at the table. She glanced slyly at Sorcha. 'How much do you charge for your services?' she asked.

Sorcha shrugged her skinny shoulders. 'I don't charge anything,' she said.

'So, I'm interested,' continued Roxanne. 'Are you employed by Nick?'

'That's right.'

'Then, he must pay you something, surely?'

Sorcha looked uncomfortable at this line of questioning. 'I just... help him out with stuff,' she said, evasively. 'No money ever changes hands.'

'Sorcha and Nick go back a long way,' said Allie, trying

to be helpful. 'He helped her out with something years ago and she's paying him back.'

Roxanne looked troubled by this explanation. 'Sounds a bit like slavery to me,' she observed.

'It's not a million miles away from that,' admitted Sorcha, flatly. 'Except with slavery, there's always one sure way out of it. The way this works, I'm sort of tied in.' She turned to leave. 'If you need anything I'll be in the lounge,' she said. She threw a challenging look at Roxanne. 'Watching *The Canteen*, on Dave,' she added and went out, before Roxanne could reply.

Allie sipped her coffee. 'Don't pay any attention to her,' she said. 'She's a grumpy cow sometimes.'

'Oh, that's OK,' said Roxanne. 'I suppose I should be flattered, really. I'm amazed they're still showing that old thing.' She lifted a slice of toast to her mouth and chewed for a while. 'How come Sorcha never eats?' she asked.

'I think it's just that she prefers to eat at night, when everyone's gone to bed,' said Allie.

'Hmm.' Roxanne seemed unconvinced by the answer. 'There's something here that doesn't make sense,' she said. 'I can't quite put my finger on it, but Nick has some kind of a hold on her, doesn't he?'

Allie shrugged. 'I think they're just very old friends,' she said.

'No, that's not it at all. They strike me as the opposite of friends. It's almost as if he's got something on her. Like he's blackmailing her or something...' She broke off and glanced at her watch. 'Hey, look at the time!' she exclaimed. 'We need to be at the theatre in fifteen minutes.' She turned her attention to her food and started shovelling in huge mouthfuls of toast and egg.

'Take it easy,' Allie told her. 'It won't matter if we're a few minutes late.'

'I know, but,' Roxanne broke off in mid-sentence as something seemed to catch in her throat. Her eyes bulged. She stood up from the table and coughed convulsively, retched, spat the food back onto her plate. Her face darkened to a deep red and she coughed a second time, grabbed a glass of water from the table and gulped it down.

'Are you all right?' Allie asked her.

Roxanne shook her head, cleared her throat. She opened her mouth to reply but nothing came out. She stared at Allie in alarm and lifted a hand to her throat. She coughed a third time – a harsh, grating sound, as though something was stuck in her gullet, then tried once more to speak, but she couldn't seem to form any words.

'Roxanne?' said Allie. 'What's wrong with you?'

Now Roxanne grabbed her empty glass, ran to the sink and filled it from the tap. She drained its contents, cleared her throat loudly and raggedly. She tried to speak again, failed, shook her head, drank more water, tried a third time. She gave another hacking cough and then suddenly, shockingly, a thick spray of crimson spurted from her mouth into the sink.

'Oh my God!' Allie ran across to her and stared horrified into the bowl, which was now covered in thick pools of blood. Allie's eyes bulged. Something was moving in that blood – little fat wriggling things that looked like maggots. She stepped back with a gasp of revulsion and turned to stare at Roxanne, realising that she had registered the creatures too. Her face had gone a deathly white. She slammed the glass down on the draining board with such force it shattered into fragments, and then turned to face Allie. A selection of expressions moved across her face –

astonishment, fear, panic, then outright terror. She seemed to make a decision. She reached into her pocket and pulled out her mobile phone. As Allie watched, she opened up the contacts, her hand shaking. She clicked on one of them and handed the phone to Allie.

'What do you want me to do?' gasped Allie. Roxanne waved her hands in agitation and pointed to the display. Allie saw that she had dialled a taxi service. Allie lifted the phone to her ear and heard a woman's voice asking her politely what she wanted. It had been so long since Allie had used a phone, the process seemed odd.

'We need a taxi,' she said. 'As soon as possible, please.' And she gave her address. Her own voice sounded as though it was coming from hundreds of miles away because it had just suddenly struck her what the possible implications of this were. And they were terrifying.

'And where would you like to go?' asked the voice.

Allie glanced at Roxanne and saw the desperation in her eyes.

'The nearest hospital,' said Allie flatly. 'As fast as you can.'

22

A & E

Allie sat on a chair in the hospital corridor, desperately telling herself that everything was going to be alright. Sorcha sat next to her, gazing abstractedly into space, bored. As usual, she'd insisted on accompanying the other two in the cab, and all the way to the Royal Infirmary, she'd asked a series of dumb questions.

'What's the matter with you?' she kept asking Roxanne. 'Can't you say anything? Can't you speak? Christ, what are you going to do about tonight?'

Allie had tried quietening her down, but she kept right on asking the questions – almost as though she was secretly enjoying this.

'Did something get stuck in your throat? Is it because you were eating your breakfast too quickly?'

Once at A&E, there'd been a short, agonising wait before Roxanne was whisked away on a wheelchair to an emergency room, and now there was nothing to do but sit, hoping for good news, hoping that a doctor would appear and announce that Roxanne's voice had returned as suddenly and mysteriously as it had disappeared – and yet, somehow, Allie knew that wouldn't be the case. This was clearly Nick's work and he had timed it perfectly to create the maximum amount of trouble. Before she'd gone into the emergency room, Roxanne had dialled David's number on her mobile and then handed the phone to

Allie, clearly wanting her to explain why the two of them weren't at the theatre. Needless to say, David had gone ballistic when Allie had explained their absence. He'd started shouting and swearing, until Allie had finally been obliged to hang up on him – but not before she'd told him where she was. So she wasn't really surprised when David arrived, looking hot and extremely harassed. He saw Allie sitting in the corridor and hurried over to her.

'Will somebody please tell me what the hell is going on?' he barked.

'I thought I did,' said Allie. 'Roxanne has lost her voice.'

'But what do you mean she's lost it? Does she have a cold or something? Laryngitis? How can somebody just lose their voice?'

'I've no idea! She was eating her breakfast and I think something got stuck. She's with the doctor now.'

'Well, can I go in and see her?'

'No, not yet. They said we had to wait until they've had a chance to properly examine her.'

David gave a sigh of exasperation, but he slumped into the chair beside Allie. 'This is a nightmare,' he said to the corridor at large. 'It couldn't have happened at a worse time. We've got a sold-out theatre tonight.' He shook his head, then looked sharply at Allie. 'You realise, if she can't appear, you'll have to go on in her place?'

Allie stared at him. 'Oh no,' she said, 'I don't think so.'

'Well, of course you will! You're her bloody understudy, aren't you?'

'But what about my part?'

'Oh, we can assign that to one of the Uni girls. It's only a few lines, they'd jump at the chance. But you agreed to understudy Roxanne, didn't you?'

'Yes, that's true, but I never thought…'

'I said it was a mistake,' continued David, as though talking to himself now. 'I told Roxanne you weren't experienced enough, but she insisted. Said you knew the part perfectly.' He looked at her again. 'Please tell me that's true,' he snarled.

'Oh, well it is, but, I didn't think it would ever come to this.'

'Well, maybe I'm getting ahead of myself,' reasoned David. 'I mean, she could come out here any minute and be absolutely fine. Couldn't she?' He thought for a moment. 'Tell me again what happened.'

'We'd been for our morning run,' said Allie. 'Like we always do. Sorcha had made scrambled eggs.'

'And wholemeal toast,' Sorcha reminded her.

'Yes, and toast, and we were eating and Roxanne realised we were running late, so she started to shovel it down. I told her to take it easy. And suddenly, it was like some food seemed to stick in her throat or something. She coughed it straight up again, but then she couldn't get any words out.'

'You haven't mentioned the blood,' Sorcha reminded her.

'Blood?' David looked shocked.

'She coughed up some blood,' admitted Allie. She decided not to mention the wriggling things she'd seen within it.

David shook his head. 'It's a nightmare,' he said again. 'I mean, what are the odds?'

'Maybe it's some kind of a curse,' said Sorcha.

David glared at her. 'What are you talking about?' he snapped.

'Well, this play's about witchcraft, isn't it?' Sorcha gave him a flat stare. 'Maybe there's a curse on it.'

210

David looked at Sorcha as though he could cheerfully strangle her. 'That's really not very helpful,' he told her.

'It wasn't meant to be,' Sorcha assured him. 'I'm only saying.'

'Yes, well, thanks for your input,' said David, sarcastically. 'I'll bear it in mind.' He stared at his hands as though he really was considering putting them around Sorcha's throat.

Sorcha looked like she might be thinking about saying something else but, luckily, she was interrupted by the arrival of a young doctor, dressed in a white coat. She studied the group for a moment. 'Are you all here for Miss Walsh?' she asked.

'Yes,' said David. 'What's the news, Doctor?'

The woman shook her head. 'I'm afraid it's not good,' she said. 'Her voice is completely gone. And until we carry out more tests, I have no clue what's happened to her. It's as though her vocal cords have ruptured.'

David stared. 'But how could that happen?' he cried.

'I really have no idea. I've never come across anything like it before. Her larynx has been severely traumatised. We gave Miss Walsh a writing pad and she wrote that she choked on some food. Is that right?'

'Scrambled egg,' said Allie.

'And toast,' added Sorcha. 'Wholemeal toast.'

'I think something got stuck in her throat,' said Allie. 'But it was only for a moment. She coughed it straight out again.'

'I have to admit I'm stumped,' said the doctor. She looked puzzled. 'She wrote something else on the pad, the word "maggots". Does that mean anything to any of you?'

Allie frowned. 'Well, she coughed some blood into the sink and it did look like something was moving in the blood. Little wriggling things.'

'Jesus,' said David.

'That's not possible,' the doctor assured him. 'Really. Must have been bits of food. We'll know more when we've had a chance to carry out some tests.'

'How long will that take?' demanded David.

'Well, I can't say for sure. We should have answers some time tonight.'

David slumped back in his seat and stared imploringly up at the ceiling. He groaned. 'It can't be tonight,' he said. 'Tonight she's supposed to be on the stage of the Lyceum!'

'I appreciate this isn't what you want to hear,' continued the doctor. 'And I'm well aware who the patient is. But look, the kind of damage she's endured… well, it could be months before she can speak again. Possibly longer. I suppose there must be some kind of backup plan for this kind of thing?'

David nodded sullenly and sat, staring off into space.

'Well,' said the doctor. 'At any rate, I need to get on. You can go in and see her briefly, but try not to stay too long. As I'm sure you can appreciate, she's pretty emotional right now.' She pointed to the open doorway of a side ward. 'She's straight through there. I've explained to her that she'll have to stay here tonight for observation. Obviously, she's upset, so go easy on her.' She gave them what was probably intended to be an encouraging smile. 'Good luck with the show,' she added. She nodded and moved away along the corridor.

Allie and David stood up but Sorcha remained where she was. 'You guys go ahead,' she muttered. 'I'll wait here.' She paused, then directed a sardonic smile at Allie. 'Give her my love,' she said, and Allie had the distinct conviction that Sorcha had somehow known that this was going to happen.

Allie headed into the ward and David trudged along behind her, looking like a man who had just been sentenced to a long time in prison. They found Roxanne slumped in a wheelchair, looking desperately sorry for herself. Her eyes were red from crying and when she saw her two visitors fresh tears brimmed and trickled down her face, but weirdly, no sounds came from her other than gasps. Allie went straight over and put her arms around Roxanne. 'I'm so sorry,' she whispered. David hung back at a polite distance, his expression grim.

Allie straightened up and saw that Roxanne had the writing pad and biro on her lap. As Allie watched, Roxanne took the pen and wrote on the pad, then turned it around so Allie could read it.

BREAK A LEG, it said.

Allie shook her head. 'Oh, no,' she said. 'No, no, there must be some other way! This isn't right. It's your role.'

Roxanne shook her head. She turned the pad around again and wrote.

YOU'LL BE GREAT.

'But I won't,' insisted Allie. 'I shouldn't have let you talk me into the understudy thing in the first place. Really, I'm just a kid. You're... you're Roxanne Walsh.'

In reply, Roxanne simply underlined the last thing she'd written and held it up so that Allie could read it. Then she reached out and took Allie's hands in hers, looked up at her imploringly.

'I can't!' sobbed Allie.

Roxanne released her hold and wrote on the pad a third time.

I BELIEVE IN YOU, it said.

She looked meaningfully at David and he seemed to understand. He nodded. 'Right,' he muttered. 'I'll get straight back to the Lyceum and explain to everyone what's happening. I'll leave you two alone for a few minutes – but Allie, get over to the theatre as soon as you can. We need to run through the whole script with you as Abigail.'

Allie nodded, realising as she did so that her own eyes were filling with tears. She waited until David was gone before she turned back to Roxanne.

'You don't understand,' she said. 'You don't know what you're asking of me. People will have come expecting to see you. They'll hate me!'

Roxanne shook her head and underlined the last thing she'd written; then she added several exclamation marks to it. She couldn't know, of course, what she was really asking Allie to do. Nick had been so clever, so devious. If Allie took this role, she would be fulfilling the terms of her contract. She'd be taking a lead role in a major theatre in Edinburgh.

'Please,' whispered Allie. 'There has to be some other way!'

But again, Roxanne shook her head and pointed to Allie. She wrote one last thing on the pad.

DO IT FOR ME. PLEASE.

Then Allie had her arms around Roxanne and the two of them were hugging each other and crying and it seemed to Allie, that, although Roxanne must be feeling devastated right now, Allie was the one who really had something to cry about.

23

THE SHOW MUST GO ON

Allie sat in the dressing room, looking at her reflection in the mirror. She was in costume for the role of Abigail Williams. She had managed to get through a fraught and nervous last run-through without totally disgracing herself and, in about fifteen minutes, she would be called to take her place in the wings, ready to walk out onto the stage. The problem was, she hadn't yet decided if she was actually going to do it. Typically, the one time she really needed to talk to Nick, there was no sign of him. She had asked Sorcha about twenty times if she had any way of summoning him, but she'd just shrugged her skinny shoulders and shaken her head.

'He'll come when he's ready,' she said.

Finally, Allie got sick of seeing Sorcha's mournful features and had banished her from the dressing room. She needed to be left alone, to consider her future, to make what would probably be the most important decision of her life.

And, typically, that was when the door opened and Nick finally strolled in, smiling like the cat who got the cream. He studied Allie's reflection in the mirror for a moment and then took a seat beside her. And that was when she saw his reflection for the first time. It was no longer the face of a young man, but an ancient, white-haired grandfather, his face lined and scored with centuries of misspent life. He grinned, revealing two rows of hideous, yellow teeth.

'Well, my dear,' he said. 'Here we are. I must say we got to it a lot quicker than I anticipated. And, it would seem, you have a decision to make.'

Allie nodded. 'I don't suppose there's any chance of a miracle recovery, is there?' she asked. 'You can't just give Roxanne back her voice and let her go on tonight as planned?'

'I really don't think that's on the cards,' said Nick. He shook his head and then made an innocent face. 'Oh wait, you think I was responsible for what happened to her? I can't help feeling a little got at. What if it was just chance? Just one of those freak things that you read about in the newspaper?'

'I don't believe that for a minute,' said Allie. 'You arranged this. You planned it down to the last detail.'

'Well, if that's what you think, then I shan't bother to argue,' said Nick.

Allie turned back to the mirror. 'I don't have to do it,' she told her own reflection. 'I don't have to go on. I could pretend to faint and then what could they do? Nothing.'

Nick chuckled. 'True enough,' he said. 'And, of course, that's entirely up to you. After all, we've only just begun this journey together.'

Allie turned to look at him, surprised by his attitude, and once again she was seeing the Nick she knew: young and devilishly handsome. 'You don't seem to care at all,' she observed.

He made a dismissive gesture with one hand. 'I play the long game,' he told her. 'If you pass up this opportunity, I'll create another one. And another. And another, until finally we arrive at the one thing you really cannot resist.

It's called temptation, Allie, and it's my stock-in-trade – the one thing you humans cannot ultimately resist. So, if it's not this play that gets you, it will be something else – a film role, a chance to date the boy you've always wanted, a dream holiday in the sun, the chance to be a best-selling novelist... oh, there are so many things I can offer you, my girl. And after all, there's no great hurry. I have all the time in the world. Maybe I won't get you until you're old and grey. I can think of a handful of people who have managed to elude me for that long. But they are few and far between.'

Allie swallowed. 'And if I do go out on that stage?' she murmured. 'What happens to me after that?'

Nick chuckled. 'I don't believe you really want to know the answer to that,' he said. 'Suffice to say, it won't be the most pleasant experience of your life. And it will go on for eternity.'

'Like Sorcha?' murmured Allie.

'Oh, well, that's a slightly different arrangement,' said Nick. 'Sorcha took her own life, you see, which means she belongs in the world of the undead. She must simply wait on me for the rest of time. To my mind, that's something she should be absolutely thrilled about. But she doesn't seem the least bit grateful.'

'Because she wants out of the agreement.'

Nick shrugged. 'Tough luck,' he said. 'She too is in it for the long haul.'

Allie considered for a moment. 'What if we were to make another deal?' she asked Nick.

He sniggered. 'Forgive me, but you're really in no position to make any kind of deal,' he said. 'You signed the contract. There's no getting out of that.'

'I wasn't thinking of me,' Allie assured him. 'I was thinking about Sorcha.'

Nick scowled. 'What about her?' he snarled.

Allie looked him straight in the eye. 'What if I agree to go out on that stage with one condition?'

Now Nick looked interested. 'And what condition is that?' he asked.

'That if I perform tonight, you let Sorcha go. You let her die. And you agree never to use her again.'

Nick tilted his head to one side, clearly intrigued. 'Are you honestly telling me that you'd put somebody else's welfare above your own?'

'I might. If I had your promise that you wouldn't go back on the deal.'

Nick chuckled. 'How very noble,' he said. 'Forgive me, but I'm fascinated. It's so rare for a human to place another person's plight above their own. Why is this so important to you?'

'Because I've worked with Sorcha, I've seen how miserable she is, how lonely. You've had her working for you since the eighteen-hundreds. Surely all people get to retire one day?'

'Not when they work for me!' snapped Nick. 'Like I told you, I play the long game.' He seemed to consider for a moment. 'But, then again, she's of no consequence,' he said. 'I have thousands just like her. Millions! It's not as if she would be any great loss. And she is particularly annoying.' He looked around the room, weighing things up. 'What if I agreed to grant your condition? How do I know you'll keep your side of the bargain?'

Allie pondered the matter for a few moments. 'I could do the performance first and you could let her watch. You'd have to promise that straight afterwards, you'd do whatever is needed to... to...'

'Terminate her employment?' suggested Nick.

'Exactly. I'd need you to swear to me you'd do it.'

Nick seemed suddenly rather cross. 'I resent the suggestion that I am not a man of honour,' he said. 'If I tell you I shall do something then I shall indeed do it! I'm not somebody who ever goes back on his word.'

'Say it then,' suggested Allie.

'Really?' He made a face, as though she was asking a lot of him – but after a few moments, he began to speak in a slow, considered tone. 'I promise that if Allie Lawrence performs in *The Crucible* tonight, on the stage of the Lyceum Theatre, Edinburgh, then I shall liberate her companion, Sorcha–' He looked puzzled. 'I can't seem to remember her second name,' he said.

'It doesn't matter, we both know who you mean,' said Allie.

'Oh, so you'll trust me that far then? How very generous of you.' Nick smirked, then shrugged his shoulders. 'I shall liberate Sorcha and send her into the darkness of death, where I can exercise no more dominion over her.' He spread his hands. 'There,' he said. 'I trust that will suffice?'

Allie nodded. 'That's good enough for me,' she told him. 'Just remember, if you go back on this, then our contract won't be binding anymore.'

He seemed amused by this. 'I love the way you're telling me what to do,' he said. 'I seem to remember that I hold all the cards here.'

There was a tap on the door. It opened and a young male stagehand popped his head into the room.

'Ten minutes, Miss Lawrence,' he said.

'Be right with you,' she said and he closed the door again.

Now Nick seemed puzzled. 'As easy as this?' he

murmured. 'Really? I honestly thought you'd put up more of a fight. I must say, it's a bit disappointing when you make it so easy for me.'

'Do most people put up a fight?' asked Allie.

'A lot of them try. But I have to say I expected more from you. Takes all of the fun out of it, somehow, when you just... acquiesce. '

Allie shrugged. 'I guess you were right,' she said. 'Starring in *The Crucible* has always been my dream. But, you already knew that, didn't you? How did you get them to do it, by the way? The theatre.'

'Oh, I can't take any credit for that. It was already scheduled to be the next production. Just a happy coincidence, nothing more.'

'See, I don't even know if that's the truth.'

'What reason would I have to lie to you? Sometimes, things fall into place. And sometimes, they have to be... manipulated.'

She thought for a moment. 'You know, I was thinking,' she said. 'One of the first times we talked, you said that you knew Arthur Miller. And when I said you surely weren't old enough, you changed your story. But I'm thinking now, you probably did know him, didn't you?'

He shrugged. 'What of it?' he said.

'I was just wondering. What was his price? What was the one thing he couldn't say no to?'

Nick seemed to be trying to remember. 'It was such a long time ago,' he said. 'The details are rather hazy. It could be that there was a certain American movie star he wanted me to hook him up with... but that would have just been the start. It might be that he wanted fame and fortune. And perhaps, in the end, he simply wanted to escape from the reality he found himself in – the crushing disappointment of not being quite the golden boy he once was. Sometimes that's all it takes with you creative types. But of course, I couldn't possibly comment on any of it.' He chuckled. 'At least you will be going out on a high.'

Allie got up from her chair and had a last quick glance at her reflection in the mirror. She adjusted her costume, which she had noticed was slightly wrinkled at the neck. She looked down at Nick. 'Where will we do it?' she asked. 'The last bit.'

'Here,' he said. 'Right here. When it's all over and everyone has paid their respects, as I'm sure they will all want to, I will come to this dressing room with Sorcha and we shall do what is necessary.'

'OK,' Allie said. She turned to leave but he reached out a hand and grabbed her, holding her in place. It felt like a band of ice around her wrist.

'So calm?' he asked her. 'Aren't you afraid? Aren't you trembling inside?'

'I'm trying not to think about it,' she said. 'I have my lines to remember.'

He chuckled, nodded, let go of her. 'Make it a great performance,' he advised her. 'After all, it will be your last.'

Allie looked at him for a few moments in silence. Then she went out of the room, closing the door behind her.

24

AFTER SHOW

It was like a dream, the whole thing. From the moment she stepped out into the spotlights, it was as though she was running on pure adrenalin. It coursed through her veins, making her feel totally alive, more alive than she had ever felt before. And from the moment she spoke her opening lines, she could sense that the audience was with her, hanging on to her every utterance; that they were willing her to succeed, even though they'd come to see somebody else entirely.

In the interval, various members of the cast sought her out to whisper their congratulations – even the normally aloof Olivia Quinn sidled over and gave her a whispered, 'Well done.' Rare praise indeed.

In the second half, Allie took what was left of her role, grabbed it like a terrier and shook it until it screamed for release.

There was only one point where she nearly lost it. Gazing out into the audience, midway through a long speech, she somehow managed to spot a familiar face, a beautiful woman sitting in a row about halfway back. It was Julia, her perfect features registering a melancholy smile. Thankfully, it looked as though she'd left Babette at home. Allie remembered how Sorcha had claimed that Julia preferred to stay at the old house, that she would never consider making the trip up to Edinburgh, but for some reason, this time she had. Was this her way of saying goodbye? Had she come to watch another of Nick's conquests make her swansong?

For an instant, Allie struggled to remember the next line and there was a long, uncomfortable pause, but then, somehow, the words came to her and she moved on, picking up the thread, making it seem almost as though her pause had been deliberate. There were no other problems. When the cast came out to take their bows, the audience applause was so enthusiastic, it felt as though it would raise the roof, and when the other members of the cast pushed Allie forward to take her own special bow, the packed audience actually got to their feet to ensure she knew how good they thought she had been. What felt particularly rewarding was the conviction that this time she had received no help from Nick. There were no entranced critics to rave about her performance, no spellbound audience members. This time the applause was genuine. She had smashed it.

Back in the dressing room she was visited by every other member of the cast, all of them telling her breathlessly that she had a brilliant future in the theatre ahead of her. Her parents weren't there tonight – they had planned to come later in the week – and Allie wasn't sure whether to be relieved or disappointed that they had missed her final performance. David made a point of dropping by to say that he was really looking forward to the rest of the run and that he'd like to put a few ideas to her for future projects he thought she might be perfect for. Then he took out his mobile phone.

'I just called Roxanne,' he said. 'I told her how brilliantly you'd handled it. She couldn't talk back of course, but she did send this.' And he showed Allie a photograph on his phone, a picture of a smiling Roxanne, lying in a hospital bed and holding up two thumbs for the camera.

'Oh, that's really lovely of her,' said Allie, aware of fresh tears welling. 'Let's hope she can get back to the role soon.'

'Well, if she can't, it's in safe hands,' said David, matter-of-factly. 'I think the critics are going to be very positive about this.'

'Yes, and this time it will be all my own work,' murmured Allie.

He looked puzzled. 'I beg your pardon?' he murmured.

'Oh, nothing,' she said.

'Anyway, make sure you get a good night's rest and I'll see you back here tomorrow for the next performance.'

And with that he left the room.

It was suddenly very quiet. Allie turned back to the mirror and started removing her makeup, taking her time, preparing herself as best she could for what came next. As she worked, she became aware of footsteps in the corridor outside, moving slowly closer. She took a deep breath and waited calmly.

The door opened and Nick sauntered into the room. Sorcha walked just behind him, wearing a slightly puzzled expression. Allie turned away from the mirror to look at her. She smiled. 'Did you watch the show?' she asked.

Sorcha nodded. 'I sure did. You were pretty amazing, girl, I have to say. You absolutely caned it.' She came closer and lowered her voice. 'I thought maybe we'd have had longer together,' she whispered. 'I didn't think you'd give in quite so easily.'

Allie shrugged. Then she looked past Sorcha to where Nick had settled himself into a chair. 'All right,' she said. 'Do whatever it is you have to do.'

Sorcha looked baffled now. 'What's going on?'

Nick waved a hand at Allie. 'Allie and I made an agreement,' he said. 'She agreed to do the performance on one condition. That I promised to let you go.'

'Let me go?' Sorcha pondered that for a moment as though she didn't really understand what he was saying. Then her face brightened as realisation dawned. She grinned and Allie couldn't help thinking that it was the first time she'd ever seen Sorcha look genuinely happy. 'Really?' she whispered. She looked at Allie. 'You're kidding me, right? You didn't, did you?'

Allie smiled. 'I did,' she said. 'I thought it was what you wanted.'

'You crazy gala!' cried Sorcha. 'I've never wanted anything as much as I want this, but I never thought anybody would sort it for me!' And she lunged forward and hugged Allie tightly. 'I don't know what to say,' she whispered. 'I don't know how to thank you enough.' Then she looked troubled. 'You know what it means for you?' she murmured. 'He'll have you right where he wants you. You do understand that?'

Allie nodded. 'I know,' she said. 'It's OK.' She squeezed Sorcha's hands. 'The thing is, are you ready for this?' she murmured. 'I know it's really short notice, but…'

'Are you kidding? I've been ready for the last hundred and fifty years!' She gave Allie a final fierce hug and then turned to look fearlessly at Nick. 'OK,' she said. 'Let's do this. Send me down.'

Nick sighed. 'Sometimes I think I'm just getting sentimental in my old age,' he complained. 'But, I agreed to it, so…' He raised a hand and made a grand flourish. 'You are dismissed,' he said.

As Allie watched in silent amazement, a curious thing

happened. A bright orange flame burst from Sorcha's chest and her skinny body began to shudder, vibrate, seemingly filled with some powerful internal energy. Her face twisted into an expression of agony and she let out a scream.

Allie looked accusingly at Nick. 'You didn't say it would hurt her!' she cried.

Nick shrugged. 'I have to have some fun,' he said.

Now the flame was spreading outwards and in an instant it flared into a powerful, seething rush of fire, erupting upwards and completely enveloping Sorcha. Allie took an involuntary step backwards, lifting a hand to shield her face from the heat. And then, without a sound, Sorcha exploded into a cloud of dust, tiny smouldering particles of her falling down through the air onto the floorboards and gathering in little drifts. And quite suddenly that was all that was left of Sorcha. Dust.

Allie regarded the grey drifts on the floor. 'There's no way you can ever bring her back?' she asked Nick.

'You're so suspicious,' he chided her. 'Have I ever lied to you?'

'No, not exactly,' said Allie. She felt calm now, decisive. 'But you've definitely bent the rules from time to time.'

'Well, trust me, there's not a chance she's coming back to this world,' he assured her. 'She's gone into the darkness forever.' He thought for a moment. 'Probably just as well,' he added. 'I was beginning to find her extremely irritating. And she was a smoker. I cannot abide them.' He sat back in his chair. 'Which brings me to you,' he said. 'I really cannot believe you've made it so easy for me. Is there anything you want to say before I pass sentence?'

'Not really,' said Allie.

'Very well then.' Nick raised a hand, as if to strike her.

'Oh, there is one thing actually.'

He sighed, lowered his hand. 'What?' he asked impatiently.

'The contract.'

He glared at her. 'What about it?'

'I'm not being funny, but… well… have you looked at it recently?'

He grimaced. 'Why would I do that?'

'Oh, just a thought. You remember that morning I signed it?'

He nodded, his eyes narrowing suspiciously. 'Of course I remember. I remember it perfectly. What about it?' he asked.

'Well, you were in such a hurry to get me to sign that day. I'm not sure you checked everything properly.'

'What are you talking about? What is there to check?'

'I don't suppose you have a copy of it?'

'Of course I do.' He lifted his hand again with a flourish. A sheaf of rolled paper appeared in his upraised hand.

'I'd just have a wee look at it, if I were you.'

He muttered something under his breath but unrolled the paper. 'What am I looking for exactly?' he asked.

'The place where I signed my name? I'm not sure if it's important, but…'

Nick found the page. He stared. His mouth fell open. 'Abigail Williams?' he murmured. He lifted his gaze to stare balefully at her. 'Abigail Williams?' he repeated, louder this time.

'Yes. Not sure why I wrote that. I did it on impulse, really.'

'Why you…. you little…'

'I mean, I don't know if it really counts if it's not actually my name–'

'But…'

'I mean, I know if it was a contract for something else, I'm pretty sure it would make a difference, so–'

His eyes bulged. 'You cheated me!' he hissed.

'Oh, no, not really. I wasn't thinking clearly and–'

'YOU LIED TO ME!'

Something was happening to Nick – something horrible. His face was changing from that of a handsome young man to that of some kind of ancient beast. His forehead swelled, rippled, his eyes sunk in on themselves to become beady, reptilian, glowing bright red. His jaw stretched downwards, the open mouth crammed with hideously misshapen teeth and a bloated purple tongue.

'This means it's all null and void,' he gasped, his voice now a beastly grunting sound 'You never promised me anything! You deceived me!' Now his body was growing in stature, swelling outwards, bursting out of his long coat and trousers, his head thrusting upwards on the long sinewy neck until it pushed against the ceiling. A pair of curved horns sprouted from his rippling forehead. And from his open mouth issued a noise – a great long bellow of rage.

'YOU WICKED, WICKED GIRL!'

All this Allie saw in the instant before darkness swept over her.

EPILOGUE

For the longest time she seemed to float, suspended in a thick, all-enveloping blackness, with no pinprick of light to illuminate the scene. She was dimly aware of noises all around her – growls, roars, general sounds of anger. She began to suspect that she was ill – that she'd had a stroke or a heart attack.

But then her vision focused and a kind of half-light returned. She blinked, looked around uncertainly. She was standing at a crossroads in the fading light of early evening, in a place she only vaguely recognised. An illuminated road sign indicated that it was thirty-one miles to Perth, the nearest town of any size. But how had she got here? Why was she standing by the roadside? And why did she have a rucksack slung over her back? It occurred to her then that a car had just slowed to a halt in front of her, a curious old-fashioned vehicle, the kind of thing you only ever saw in Hollywood movies. She caught a glimpse of the driver, a man wearing a peaked cap, staring at the road ahead.

Then she noticed a face peering out of the open rear window at her. It was the face of a stranger, an old man, thin, haggard-looking, his dark eyes sunken into pouches of grey, wrinkled skin, his straight white hair plastered greasily back against his skull. It occurred to her that the stranger had just spoken and was waiting for her to reply. She struggled to bring herself back to some kind of reality. She had a dim recollection of a silly little argument with her mother. She had walked out of the house for some reason. But where had she been going? What was she doing out here on this lonely road, so late in the day?

The man in the car coughed impatiently and she finally managed to focus her attention on him.

'Sorry?' she said.

He leaned closer to the window. 'I said, "Can I drop you somewhere?"'

She regarded the old man suspiciously and decided that he was not the kind of person it would be wise to accept a lift from. Something about him looked sinister, completely untrustworthy.

'No thank you,' she said firmly. 'I was just–'

He stared at her intently. 'Yes?' he asked her.

'I was just on my way home,' she said.

A cold, indifferent look came into his eyes. 'Suit yourself,' he muttered. 'Drive on, Tam.' The window rose upwards, hiding the old man's face, and the car drove sedately away into the gathering twilight.

Allie stared after it for a few moments until it had gone over the crossroads and was no more than two red taillights in the distance. She had the distinct impression that something had happened to her – something incredibly complicated. But how could that be when she'd only been standing here for a few minutes, minding her own business? She glanced at her watch. It was late and lights were coming on in the houses that lined the road.

She remembered then that she had indeed argued with Mum – something to do with Brandon – but she couldn't understand why she'd made such a fuss about it. Brandon was a jerk. She was better off without him. And those thoughts she'd had about running off to Edinburgh and 'being an actor'? Ridiculous!

Oh, she'd get there in the end. Of course she would, but right now the obvious thing to do was to hunker down, get those exams she needed and then apply to a university that specialised in drama. That would open up a world of opportunities to her. She'd been so ridiculously impatient before, but now it occurred to her that she had plenty of time: all the time in the world.

A chill breeze fluttered her hair. If she started back now, she thought, she'd be home in time for dinner. Shepherd's pie. Oh well, she felt hungry enough to eat several helpings. In fact, now she thought about it, she was ravenous. Then, for an instant, a strange image flickered through her mind's eye.

She was standing on a balcony looking out across a sunlit meadow, where people lounged on the grass, eating picnics, cooking barbecues – or they jogged or rode bicycles on a stretch of tarmac that ran alongside the grass. It was only in her mind for an instant, but while it lasted it was so real, she could almost smell the powerful scent of freshly-mown grass. And then it was gone as suddenly as it had appeared.

'What was that all about?' she muttered.

She shrugged her coat tighter around her, turned on her heel and started back in the direction of home, walking with a new sense of purpose.